SATIN A⌣ PEARLS

THE VIRGIN DIARIES

LAUREN LANDISH

Edited by
VALORIE CLIFTON
Edited by
STACI ETHERIDGE

 *iary Entry, March 4th*

DEAR DIARY,

I have a confession to make. I hate my math professor, Connor Daniels.

From the moment he walked into class, he's been a thorn in my side, constantly irritating and annoying me as he teaches. Arrogant doesn't even begin to describe him, and it burns me how he expects all of us to be just as perfect as he is, pushing us to do better, learn faster, be more like him. I get that teachers are supposed to challenge their students, but he's such a . . .

He's a dick.

Cocky. Big-headed. Egotistical.

So why can't I stop fantasizing about him? Standing up there in his tight jeans, his bulge practically flaunted in my face. I picture the victorious way he'd smirk as he bent me over the desk, flipping my skirt up and taking me. Like it was inevitable.

But here's the thing . . .

I don't want him to just take my body, or my virginity.

I want him to teach me . . . everything.

CHAPTER 1

DAISY

"*T*hat asshole!" I seethe, blindly stabbing my way through a chunk of iceberg lettuce while staring at the paper in front of me. Arianna, my best friend and dormie, nods as she shoves a cherry tomato into her mouth, letting me continue my rant. "I spent all weekend busting my butt on this, double-checked it all, and he still gave me a *C*! A freaking *C*!"

"Let me see," Arianna says, mouth still full as she snatches the paper from my hands. She stares at my paper for a bit, then shakes her head. "Seriously, a point off for not closing a parenthesis at the end of an equation, and you got the right answer? That man has it in for you."

I can't answer for a moment as I chew crunchily. "He's an asshole," I repeat when I can finally form words again.

"Mmm, but what an ass," Arianna jokes, miming spanking the air in front of her like it's Professor

LAUREN LANDISH

Daniels's butt. The bad thing is she's right. He's like the prettiest gift under the Christmas tree, all sexy and smart, but when you open it, *wah-wah* . . . the most frustrating personality.

"What?" I gasp. "Did you *really* just say that?"

Arianna, who's the sort where you're not sure whether she's joking or not, nods. "Well, he's hot as hell. I'm jelly, girl. If there's anyone who can make math interesting, it's that man. I'd be studying more than I have my entire life and asking for after-hours help!"

I open my lips to object but close my mouth. The fact is, Ari's right. Professor Daniels is the hottest professor—check that, the hottest man on campus. And I haven't told her about how I fantasize about him almost every night. I can't. It'd be impossible to explain how I can both hate him and lust after him, all at the same time. I don't even understand it myself.

"After-hours help? Fuck, you're right. I need to go to tutoring, don't I? Noooo." My head falls as the realization rings true.

"Yeah, well," Arianna says with a smile, "that wouldn't be all bad, now would it? And a *C* isn't going to cut it, girly. Math is your major, after all, and he's got influence in the department. You'd better make a good impression on him."

I don't really have an answer. What *am* I going to do? It doesn't seem as simple as 'study more'. Couldn't hurt, but shit, I already do more than most, and he always finds some way to dock my score. Admitting to needing help rubs me the wrong way, but Arianna's right. If I'm

4

going to continue on with my Master's or a PhD, I could use a recommendation from Professor Daniels.

But since the first day in his class, he's been on my ass. Not literally, of course. That might actually be fun. I'd like to think it's because he recognized right away that I could take it, that I would be one of his better students and he needed to push me. But if that's the case, it damn sure doesn't feel like it. And at this point, the grades are starting to catch up to me and I'm doubting my love of math, something that's always been steadfast for me.

I need that feeling back . . . that everything is logical, rational, and makes sense if you follow the step-by-step rules to find the solution. He's taken that from me, and if swallowing my pride and asking for some additional help will get me back on solid ground, I'll do it.

Secretly, I'll admit there's a part of me that thinks being alone in a room with Professor Daniels sounds pretty sweet. Beyond the help to get my grade up, something I desperately need to do, the fantasy fodder is enticing.

"Ugh, fine. I'll go by his office," I say, rolling my eyes as I beg the fluorescent cafeteria lights for strength. "What about you? Have you gotten that internship at Morgan yet?" I ask Arianna, trying to change the subject. Talking about Professor Daniels both annoys me and makes me hot, neither of which I want right now.

She takes the bait, thankfully. "Nope. Haven't heard a word back. I heard they're doing a reorganization, which is slowing the whole thing down. Until they get that straightened out, they're sitting on their asses."

I hum sympathetically, shaking my head. Ari's been dying to get her foot in the door at Morgan. Me, I've just been focusing on my grades, trying to make sure they're where they need to be to get into graduate school when the time comes. Might sound boring, but I want to control my own research, so that's what I'll need.

"Well, I'm sure you'll hear back," I reassure her. "You've got great ideas on just about everything."

"Just about?" Arianna asks, and I shrug.

"Depends on what you say we're doing this weekend," I challenge.

And just like that, she's off and running down a list of possible activities for the weekend. None of which include my going to private, one-on-one, after-hours tutoring with a man totally off limits, completely maddening, and sexy as fuck.

"SO CLASS, WHEN YOU'RE LOOKING AT THE APPLICATION of the cosine function to this curve . . ." Professor Daniels says. He continues talking, but my mind is wandering, perusing his body, every inch the dream that constantly haunts my sleep.

His thick slabs of muscle seem out of place on a man who knows more about math than all but maybe a couple of dozen people in the world. And today, he's showing off. He's always shunned the traditional 'academics' garb. In fact, the only day I've ever seen him in a jacket and tie was the first day of class, and today, he's decided to go even more casual, in a Batman T-shirt and jeans that hug his ass so well.

Could he be a smart and sexy *nerd*? The thought of him as a fanboy at a Comicon strikes me as funny until I think of what costume he might wear. I imagine how a skin-tight Batman suit would look on Daniels's perfectly sculpted body.

The thought engulfs my brain, and I can barely pay attention to what he's saying every time he turns around to write on the board. I don't even notice that I'm nibbling on the eraser of my pencil as he talks, my eyes glued to him.

Luckily, I'm in the front row, right where the best students always sit. I'm not an ass-kisser, teacher's pet type, but I definitely know myself. And if I sit in the back, I'll spend the whole class watching people type on their phones, play video games on their laptops, and grab at whatever other distractions catch my attention. Up front, I get none of that and my focus stays exactly where it should be.

Unfortunately, Professor Daniels mostly ignores me. He only calls on me when I don't know the answer, studiously overlooking me when I do raise my hand. Speaking of, I realize he just asked a girl in the back a question. I turn to look as she answers correctly.

"Yes, Miss Jacobs. That's correct," Professor Daniels says from the front of the room. The brunette beams like she answered the million-dollar question, placing a hand on her chest . . . her very visible, cleavage-pressed-up-to-her-chin chest. She's one of *those*.

For the most part, the girls in the room dress one of two ways—either total college girl, don't-give-a-fuck attire, complete with yoga pants, baggy T-shirts, and messy hair, or bordering on night-out gear, tight jeans or short skirts, low-cut tops, and a full face of makeup at ten A.M. I feel certain those outfits are strictly for Daniels's benefit.

I'm somewhere in the middle, not overdoing it but putting forth some effort to look pulled together. Today, I have on skinny jeans and a V-neck shirt. Nothing too fancy, although I'd admit that I have on my favorite bra, the one that makes my tits look phenomenal without going too overboard. Classy sexy. Even though it's wrong, a small part of me hopes he'll notice.

So far, no dice.

Of course.

My eyes are drawn to his crotch as he turns back around. Have mercy, what I would do to see what he's got lovingly cradled in those Levi's. Okay, so I might not know exactly what to do with it even if I could see, but I'm sure I'd figure it out really fucking quick. I'm a virgin, not a nun, and I've definitely seen my share of adult videos and read some racy books. I wonder how he looks. Feels. Tastes.

He looks at me just as I lick my lips, and I quickly tear my eyes away, my heart pounding. Did he see me? A part of me *hopes* he saw it, and another part is afraid he'll mark down my grades even worse for my audacity. I feel a flush rush across my cheeks as I cross my legs, squeezing my thighs to get some relief so I can focus.

"So now, please clear your desks for the exam," Professor Daniels says, picking up a pile of papers. "I'll leave these review notes on the board. Some of you could use the boost."

He goes down the front row, silently counting off a pile of papers before handing them to us to pass back. When he reaches me, he pauses, his eyes looking into mine for a moment, and I freeze like a deer in headlights. Oh, God, he totally saw me. I'm so busted, and the embarrassment has me biting my lip, scared he's actually going to call me out in front of everyone.

There's a hint of a smirk on his sensuous lips, but he hands me eight copies of the test to send back without a word. Then he moves on, leaving behind nothing but the spicy presence of his cologne like a ghost to mirror my own arousal.

I watch as he moves the rest of the way down the front row, his commanding presence a draw for my eye as much as his ass in those jeans. Then he moves to the front of the room, sitting down on the desk like he's the fucking boss. I guess in this room, he is.

Face it, Daisy. He's so sexy, there's a reason none of the boys around here interest you. He's a real man, my inner voice says, *one who could show you just what you've been missing.*

Damn it! Focus, Daisy!

I'm in so much trouble. I'm supposed to be concentrating on math, but my mind replays the moment when he caught me staring at his crotch, wondering about how big his dick is. In my imagination, I don't blush like the semi-clueless virgin I am. Instead, I beckon him over and he unzips for me, letting his thick cock peek out of his jeans, and I lean forward, pressing my tits to the desk to taste him. And he groans at the delicious sensation, grabbing handfuls of my hair to guide me as he fucks my mouth.

"Fuck me," I mutter to myself, not sure if I'm talking about my fantasy or my outlook for this test.

Daniels looks at his watch, a huge Rolex that speaks to his appreciation of the finer things in life. "You may begin. Good luck," he says as time starts.

"I can do this. I've studied and I know this material. Slow and careful and I'll get that *A*," I whisper, turning over my test sheet. Ugh.

Time to get to work. I can't waste precious seconds worrying about how far down my throat I could take Professor Daniels's cock. That's tangential to my current situation. "Just a sine of the times," I joke to myself, hoping the math jokes get me going.

I work meticulously, double-checking every answer once I'm done to make sure every decimal point is where I want it and that I haven't made any stupid mistakes . . . like leaving out a parenthesis. Yeah, I've learned my lesson. When I'm done, there are still twenty minutes left in class, and I nod to myself. "Okay. I've got this."

I look around. Everyone still has their heads buried in their papers, but there's nothing else for me to do. I should feel good, but it kind of worries me that I'm done so much faster than anyone else. I did check over it, though. I consider going over it again to fill time, but

I'm nervous I'll overthink things and change correct answers.

Putting my pencil away, I look up at Professor Daniels, who's moved to the stool behind his desk and is sitting with his feet up on the bar, his powerful thighs stretching the denim of his jeans as he lords over the domain of his classroom, watching us work.

I walk up, laying my paper on the desk in front of him.

Professor's eyes follow my approach. I notice that his gaze falls into the lightly tanned valley between my breasts for an instant, and heat floods my body before he jerks them away, reaching over to pick up his red pen as he glares at my paper like it's filthy trash.

"That was quick. Are you sure you're done?" he asks. His tone is questioning, like he already knows I fucked this up. I square my shoulders, meeting his eyes defiantly. His dark look seems to burn into my very soul. And for a moment, I think he's not talking about the test . . . but that's just wishful thinking.

"I'm sure. It was hard, but I managed. I think the last one taught me to be extra-vigilant about the details," I reply so sweetly, so innocently, as if he doesn't piss me off for his anal-retentive grading. I also emphasize the *hard* a little bit too much on purpose, flirting just enough.

He smirks, nodding as his eyes take me in again. Is he actually checking me out? Heat starts to warm my core at the thought. "That's good. I'll see you next time, or just have a seat if you want to see your grade before you leave."

"Thank you, sir," I reply softly. "I hope it meets your . . . expectations."

I return to my seat, making as much of a show as I can of the few steps, letting my hips sway a little more than usual. When I sit down, I see he's still looking at me, but only for a brief moment before he turns to my paper.

I can only dream that behind his stern look, he's thinking of ways to mark me like he's marking my paper. Wait . . . what? Fuck. He just made a red mark on my test . . . and another.

Where I had been feeling sexy, my panties dampening with desire from even the momentary conversation with him, now I'm pissed anew.

Tests filter in through the rest of the time, and after they're all in, he passes out the few he's managed to grade so far. He comes by, setting my test facedown on my desk, and my hands tremble as I flip it over to find . . . a *B*.

Shocked, I go over my test, seeing the blotches of red like accusations to my intellect. My answers are correct, but it's in the here and there that he takes off the points, little errors that don't even affect the final answers!

"I'll see you all next time. I'll have the rest of the tests graded and ready to return then," he says as almost everyone files out. I gather my stuff, holding in my anger. At Daniels or myself, I'm not really sure.

"Hey, a *B*'s not too bad," a sweet voice next to me says encouragingly. I look to my right and see Sabrina Bowen. She's a junior and one of the prettiest girls in class, with long blonde hair, big blue eyes, and pouty pink lips. Pretty, smart, and sweet. If it wasn't for that last one, the sweet factor, I'd hate her out of sheer catty jealousy. But she's truly a nice person, which makes you feel like shit for being envious of her. She slides her bag over her shoulder. "I'm just hoping for a *C*."

"Thanks. Just thought I did better than this. Some of these marks are nit-picky considering I got the right answer. He's such a hardass!" I grumble, my voice getting a tad too loud by the end of my rant. She frowns sympathetically, but then I hear it.

"Excuse me?" Professor asks, looking up from another test that looks even bloodier than mine, his voice strained with cold fury. "Miss Phillips, if you'd like to protest your grade, feel free to come by my office." He caps his pen, his green eyes blazing, like he's daring me.

From beside me, I hear Sabrina slinking away and realize she's left me alone as she tries to get out of firing range.

I muster up a half-smile, feigning apology at my words, even though I'm not sorry. I'm annoyed, at him for the hypercritical grade and at myself for missing the damn details again. But I nod. Damn right, I'm coming by his office. Already planned on it.

CHAPTER 2

*S*itting down on the stool behind my desk, I don't think I've ever tried so hard to fight a hard-on. I feel like I'm trying to swim upstream in a raging river because my blood is pumping down to my cock, leaving my brain woefully unprepared. I'm trying to think of the most *unsexy* things I can to keep from tenting in my jeans. I mentally run through the prime numbers, getting to 3,083 before losing track and starting over again. Even still, I'm at half-mast, and the only relief I have is that my dick's held captive by the tightness of my jeans.

Why the fuck did I have to wear these damn jeans on the day when I knew *she'd* be in class? Should've chosen loose slacks or even sweatpants with tight boxer briefs to hide the effect she has on me. It's not like anyone cares about the professors' dress code. Hell, Professor Williams teaches in legit pajamas on occasion and nobody bats an eye, simply calling him eccentric. But no, I'm getting choked by my own jeans, pulling my favorite tee down low to hopefully hide my hardening cock.

It's because of *her*.

Daisy Phillips, sweet brown eyes hidden behind cute plastic frames, raven's-wing black hair, and curves that my hands want to explore every time I see her.

At least once a week, she makes my dick so hard it fucking hurts and I have to excuse myself for a quick run to my office to handle matters. It's more than her looks, although she's absolutely stunning. It's that she's fucking brilliant, but raw and untrained, her skills failing her potential when she rushes ahead for the answers without a care for the process. But I can help break her of that.

I'll admit there's a piece of me that is attracted to her sweet innocence too. If I were a betting man, I'd lay odds in Vegas that Daisy Phillips is a virgin. She doesn't come across as clueless, but there's something in the way she behaves, like when she flirts but is then surprised at the words coming out of her mouth. She unconsciously seems to lean forward when I teach, like untouched territory begging me to claim it.

I know it shouldn't matter. But still, the prospect of teaching her more than just math, of showing her just what her virgin pussy is capable of, leaves me almost panting for breath.

The clock ticks away, marking off the seconds of exquisite torture as I yearn for her eyes to come back to me, but she stays dutifully focused on her test. I bury my head in some other work, rereading and double-checking a paper I'm submitting to a big mathematics journal. I don't mind publishing and the popularity contest it can be, but it's not my passion. However, I need to publish more if I'm going to get the tenured position I'm looking for. Dean Michaels is a bit of a stickler, and if I want him to consider me seriously, I've got to continually publish, not rest on my laurels from the kudos on my last paper. Even though it's the one that got me hired on as a full-time professor.

But they don't hand tenure to a professor who has his cock buried in his student's pussy, no matter how tight or sweet it might be, I remind myself.

I hear a squeak of a shoe on tile and the light footsteps as someone approaches my desk, but I can tell without looking up who it is. I've come to almost memorize every detail about Daisy, from the luster of her hair in the light of the classroom to the soft, feminine smell that is undeniably her. It's so unique and intoxicating that I can't even think of the damn flower the same way any longer. She's invaded my mind just like the beautiful weed she's named after, wild and unassuming as she overtakes my every sense.

Still, I do my best to keep my face impassive as she stands in front of me, pausing for a moment before putting her test paper down. I know my eyes freeze as I take in the lush mounds of her breasts in that daring V-cut top she's teasing me with today, and I have to struggle to keep my voice sounding bored. "That was quick. Are you sure you're done?"

She does her best to seem sweet and innocent when she answers, but I can tell she's got something else on her mind. The dirty emphasis on the *hard*, the flush in her cheeks . . . all it makes me think of is bending her over her desk, pulling those undoubtedly good-girl panties aside, and slamming my cock balls-deep in her over and over until I give her pussy its first taste of how it feels to be fucked.

Dammit. My hot gaze follows her ass as she walks to her desk, turns around, and sits down. Even worse than my doing that is that she catches me, I'm sure of it.

At her haughty look, a challenge if ever I saw one, my cock surges to full hardness, forcing me to stifle a groan as I squeeze my eyes shut to try and focus before turning my attention to her test.

As always, her work is damn-near perfect. I have to study her test to find any flaws, for anything she could improve on. Part of me knows I'm being unfair to her and that I'm punishing her for cockteasing me, even if she's unaware of the consequences of her casual flirting.

But consciously, I tell myself that I expect perfection. She's so talented, the sort of mind that, if developed, could do great things. So I push, finding the imperfections in her answers. I could just mark it and not take any points off, but that's not how you learn. She needs the challenge, the ding to her status-quo easy-*A* life because she needs to *learn*.

Other students pass in papers as the test time wraps up, and I work to get as many graded as I can. Once they're all on my desk, I hand out the few I've finished to the students who chose to stay and see their grades.

When everyone files out, I sit at my desk, fighting the

last vapors of my desire for Daisy and forcing my eyes to the test in front of me, giving each student's work the attention it deserves. Even so, my ears are trained on Daisy's soft voice as she complains to another student. I know students bitch about their grades, but I'm surprised to hear her mouthiness, especially while still in my classroom.

"Excuse me?" I ask, looking up to glare at her. Her eyes are wide, her face flushed at being called out. I want to smack her bratty ass, make her apologize for her insolence on her knees with my cock in her throat. My cock screams at me to make that image a reality. Knowing it's a dangerous proposition but following protocol anyway, I offer, "Miss Phillips, if you'd like to protest your grade, feel free to come by my office." It sounds like both a threat and a promise, at least to my dirty mind.

It's obvious she's pissed, but she manages to smile and nod. I get up and motion for her to follow me to my office.

We make it to my door, and I open it, going in and leaning against the oak desk, for once not caring if she sees that I'm hard as steel in my jeans. I'm too furious at her childish outburst. She's better than that.

"You have something you want to say, Daisy?" I growl, crossing my arms over my chest. I'm going to hear her out, but I won't be a pushover.

She follows me in, closing the door behind her and plopping into the chair in front of my desk with a sigh. "I'm sorry for what I said in the classroom. I was just frustrated—*am* frustrated—with my grades. You counted off points even though the answers were correct." Her voice is tight, the anger audible.

"Correct, but not perfect. Maybe I am a bit harsh, but in this class, the final answer isn't the only thing that's important. The process is equally vital," I reply, acting as if neither her eruption nor her apology phase me. Her eyes dart down to floor at the reprimand. "May I?" I ask, holding out my hand.

She pulls the test from her bag and gives it to me, our hands brushing for the barest moment. A flash of lightning shoots through me at the touch of her soft skin, and I want more. Skin on skin, her bare body pressed underneath mine.

Forcing my eyes to the paper, I say, "Like question fifteen. You didn't give me the full answer I wanted."

"It was still the right answer," she declares, eyes meeting mine and argumentative till the end.

"Not exactly. I asked for three decimal places. You gave two." She opens her mouth to interrupt, but I talk over her, giving her a hard look. "I could've taken off more points than I did. You have to be able to follow instructions explicitly."

I pause, letting my words sink in. I can see she's beginning to get it, realizing that shortcuts and assumptions don't pay off. The value is in the tedious repetition of the work, sometimes infinitesimal numbers making all the difference in the world to the result. "You're trying to move on to the graduate level, right? You need to be better."

My words are a simple observation but weighted with expectation. One she can work to live up to or blow off and waste her potential.

Her eyes widen, her cheeks flush, and I try to sway her decision. "I'm sure you've had math teachers fawn all over you in the past, or maybe they overlooked you, trusting that you'd catch on quickly. But they didn't do you any favors, and now you're simply being lazy instead of fighting for the education you're capable of."

She's speechless and not sure how to reply at first. "What if I don't know what I'm capable of?" she asks quietly, biting her lip. I'm not sure we're talking about her math test anymore, but I do my damnedest to stay on track, even as my mind races away with thoughts of showing her what her sweet pussy can do.

I lean down, silently demanding her attention on me. "You are capable of exceptional work, Miss Phillips. This," I say, laying the test paper in her lap and fighting the urge to brush the back of my hand along her thigh, "is lazy work."

She looks down at the paper, then at me, fire in her brown eyes, "Are you this nitpicky with everyone, or do you have a problem with me?"

I shrug, disappointed that she heard the criticism more than the compliment because I don't hand those out often. "Everyone knows I'm a cocky son of a bitch and that my class is hard."

She glances down at my cock as I mention *hard* and swallows. "It is . . . hard," she murmurs, talking to my crotch. I can see her pulse racing in her neck as her chest lifts with her panting breath. Stuttering, she lifts her eyes, blinking away the thrall. "Your class . . . I mean, your class is hard."

She's flustered, but I'm stuck wondering exactly what she's thinking. I can guess the basic idea. I know when a woman wants me, but I'm desperate to know Daisy's desires—what little things turn her on, what secret spots she likes kissed, what she sounds like when she comes.

Not able to stand the pain building in my groin, I adjust myself, intentionally cupping my thick length. My voice is deeper, so gravel-filled it's almost a groan. "It is hard, but I think you can handle it. Isn't that right, Daisy? Can you handle my . . . *class*?"

She lets out a little squeaky noise then gawks at me, her innocence obvious and her desire apparent. There's a moment of anticipation where I don't know what she's going to do, the seconds ticking by like time has slowed. And then she grabs her bag, flipping her hair and virtually running from my office, her test paper fluttering to the ground.

Fuck. I pushed too far. Way too fucking far, especially considering she's my student and so far off limits. I shouldn't fantasize about her, but I do. Already rock-hard and so close to blowing, I rip open my jeans. It barely takes a brush of my hand, imagining it's Daisy's softness, before I'm coming, her test paper crumpled in my hand. I know it's wrong, but fuck, it feels so right.

CHAPTER 3

DAISY

"*H*ey there, chickee. You want to go to the Alpha Rho party?" Arianna asks, hanging out in our shared dorm common room. She's already made up her mind, it appears, effortlessly finding that perfect balance between cute and sexy in her short shorts and clingy tank top.

Any other Friday night, I might be interested. But after my last test and the confrontation Professor Daniels and I had in his office, partying with some frat guys is the last thing on my mind.

Once my head had cleared a bit from the sexy fog I'd been in, I'd replayed the whole scene over and over in my mind and one thing stuck out. Well, okay, more than one thing, but those things heat my pussy. The thing that warms my heart is that he said I'm capable of exceptional work. And I'm going to prove him right, no matter how much work it takes. "No, thanks. I'm gonna hit the books hard this weekend."

23

"Oh, come on. Are you still worried about that *B*?" she asks, shaking her head. "You know what you need, don't you? You've got your head so wrapped up about Mr. Daniels and his six-inch red pen, the only cure is Todd Smith and his eight-inch . . ."

She doesn't finish, just winks at me and waggles her eyebrows.

"Who's Todd Smith?" I ask, rolling my eyes. If she only knew. I've been dreaming about a lot more than Connor Daniels's red pen . . . and I'd swear in court that he's every bit of eight inches himself. At least.

"No one. I just made him up. The point is, you need some dick, girl. I'm not saying to go get your cherry popped, but a *little* action would set you straight. Trust me, I know."

"I bet you do," I reply, chuckling. Actually, I don't. Ari's a total mystery when it comes to her sex life. On one hand, she talks like she's slept her way down fraternity row. On the other . . . I've never really seen her with a guy. "But seriously, about the party . . . I'm just not in the mood. Mad at me?"

"No, chica," Arianna says, leaning over and patting me on the cheek. "But seriously, don't hit the books too hard, okay? You've been a ball of nerves for days. You need to relax."

"Be home by midnight," I joke as Arianna grabs her purse, heading out the door. "And I'll try!"

She gives me a serious look then smiles, closing the door

behind her. I go back to studying, but the more I try to focus on equations, the more my mind swirls and the problems on the page simply don't make sense.

I'm hours into this, frazzled and questioning myself on even the easiest of steps, something I usually know backward and forward and all around. I'm at that threshold where stupid things start to sound like brilliance. That's my only excuse for what I do next.

I log in to the university site on my laptop, clicking around until I get to Professor Daniels's online help portal. I'm planning to send him an email asking for help, timestamped with the Friday night hour, of course, to show just how dedicated I am. But when I enter the private math area, I can see that Professor Daniels is online too.

I stare at the little green dot beside his name for several long seconds, debating with myself on whether I should click it and initiate a chat. After our last private conversation, where I basically ran away like the fucking blushing virgin that I embarrassingly am, I don't know if I trust myself not to come out of this looking like a fool. I've replayed that interaction over and over in my mind, looking for any details I might have missed. He definitely busted me looking hungrily at his cock, and though I was horrified at first, I swear he was flirting with me. It wasn't so much his words, casually commenting about how hard his class was. It was his tone, turning the seemingly innocuous words into something filthy while he adjusted, no, cupped himself. In hindsight, I wish I'd been vixen enough to flirt back, maybe tell him that I could definitely handle his 'class', but no, I ran. Literally ran.

Biting my lip, I resituate my tits in my tank top, making them look their best, admitting to myself that I want to appear sexy for this man, to make him forget my earlier actions, both the bratty whining about my grade and the freakout. And before I can second-guess myself further, I click his name.

There's a moment of pause, digital beeps filling the quiet of my dorm room, and my heart races with anticipation. And then, there he is, his face filling my screen. It looks like he's at home, in an office, judging by the bookshelves behind him, and he's wearing a plain blue T-shirt that makes his eyes pop. And he's smirking big time, arrogant bastard that he is.

"Miss Phillips. Working hard on a Friday night, I see." It's exactly what I wanted him to think, that I'm a diligent, hard-working student willing to do whatever it takes to get the grades I want. It's true, but still, I want him to know that.

But suddenly, I feel rather pathetic, like I should be out with friends, and instead, I'm alone with my math book like a nerd. It brings back painful memories from high school, where nerdy girls with glasses who geek out about mathematical knot theory don't exactly get the hot guys' attention. I blush but force myself to speak. "Yes, sir. I'm working on the homework from today. I plan to spend the weekend really hitting the books."

"I'm glad to hear it, Daisy," he says softly, nodding.

Before I can stop the words, they fly from my mouth, "Did you mean it? What you said in your office?"

His relaxed posture disappears, instantly replaced with tension as he leans forward to the camera. "Did I mean *what*, exactly?"

He had said several things to me, so I get his confusion, and while maybe I would've asked about his innuendo when I began this call, right now, I ask what I really want to know, needing the reassurance. "Do you think I'm capable of exceptional work?" I ask quietly.

His lips thin, and I think for a second that he's disappointed with my answer, but then he speaks. "Daisy, I have had many students over the last few years. Most drudge through my class just to get the credit they need, while others have sparks of intelligence, typically math majors who really enjoy the class, who will likely go on to teach themselves or work in the private sector. Rarely, I see students who have a gift, for whom the numbers and theories come to life and who are able to manipulate the process in such a way that they create new methodologies. I was that type of student." His grin is all arrogance.

The buzz I'd been building, certain he was describing me, pops at his nerve. But he didn't answer my question. "And where do I fall in that spectrum, Professor?"

He chuckles, his eyebrows lifting in surprise. "Miss Phillips, you are most definitely exceptional. Do you know why I am so 'nitpicky', as you called it, about your work?" He doesn't wait for me to answer, just continues speaking like it's a class lecture. I listen raptly as if it's one as well.

"You take shortcuts, and while normally, I would simply not allow that as most students need to visually see each step, you don't need that. You jump from problem, to half-solution, to full-solution in half the steps the text-book requires. It's like forcing a child who knows how to multiply to count individual tally marks to get a total, uselessly time-consuming and unnecessary. But by skipping steps, your attention to detail must be flawless or you will miss something. That's why I'm so hard on you, Daisy." His voice is earnest, sincere.

I'm speechless, jaw hanging open in shock. I don't think I've ever received a compliment that made me feel this warm inside. And suddenly, it's not just my heart that's heating from his words. The beauty of his assessment hits me lower, deep in my core, and I blush fiercely. "Wow, thank you, Professor. No one has ever said anything like that to me. Just . . . thank you."

There's a moment of silence, both of us unsure where to go from here. Well, at least *I* don't know what to say. It seems like he's merely watching me, and I see his eyes trace from my messy bun to my bespectacled eyes to my cleavage. Suddenly, I'm damn glad I took the moment to fluff the girls before calling.

He breaks the silence, his voice husky and doing dangerous things to my body, even through the digital divide. "Is there something specific you called about tonight, Daisy?"

"Oh . . . uh, the homework!" I say, picking up my notebook and holding it to the camera. I realize a moment later that it'd been the perfect opportunity to say something flirty, but it's too late now. And really, I shouldn't be flirting with him anyway, no matter how sexy I find his intelligence, his muscled body, and okay, maybe his arrogance too. "I'm having some difficulty with problem twenty-four."

Five minutes later, he's let me talk my way to the solution, not simply giving it to me but making me work for it myself. He seems just as delighted with my correct answer as I am. "See, Miss Phillips? You're capable of great things . . . with the proper guidance, of course." He winks, softening the cocky joke.

But I'm beginning to think he's right. The right teacher is just what I need . . . in math and in other things. Maybe this is why I've never found the right guy for my first time. Granted, it's not like I ever got asked out in high school, but in college, there have been a few guys interested in me. But they always seemed so immature. Not like Professor Daniels. He seems confident, mature, like he'd know how to take care of me and teach me what I need to know.

"Thank you, sir. I think you're right. I just need the right teacher to show me, help me learn everything I'm capable of," I say softly, letting the sultriness I feel fill my voice. We're still speaking in innuendo, but there's no doubt to the offer I'm making. It's the most forward I think I've ever been, and while maybe that's ridiculous, it's the truth.

"Daisy . . ." he starts, leaning toward the camera again. I lean forward too, knowing it puts my cleavage front and center for him, wanting him to see me, to want me. He gulps, eyes narrowing and focused solely on my chest. "I'm your teacher, and anything beyond that would be inappropriate. You're so fucking sexy . . ." He stops, shaking his head, and forces his eyes to mine. "I mean, you're a lovely young woman and it would be in bad form for me to take advantage of that."

My face falls, and he cringes. "I'm sorry, Miss Phillips. You have no idea how truly sorry I am. Good night." And with one last look of longing at my tits, the screen goes black.

Shit.

I am so screwed. I basically just threw myself at my professor, who then had to let me down gently. But somewhere between the fear of what'll happen with my grades and mortification at his brush-off, I realize that he called me 'fucking sexy' in that deep, throaty growl of his. I wonder if that held more truth than his civilized, formal statement about my being a 'lovely young woman'.

The more I think about his words, his cocky wink, the way he leaned against his desk, putting his bulging cock right at my eye level, the hotter I get. The thought of his domineering, arrogant, sexy as fuck attitude gets me wet. I remember the hungry way his eyes traced my tits, like he'd love to bury his face in their lushness.

Before I even make the conscious effort to do so, my hands are tracing along my body. I have a momentary thought of appreciation that Ari will be out late, and then I give in to the fire Professor Daniels has been building in me all semester.

I pull my tank top over my head, cupping my breasts and talking to the black screen, imagining that his face is still peering back at me. "You like these, Professor? It seemed like you couldn't take your eyes off them." I trace my fingers around my nipples, gasping as I pinch their stiff peaks.

Keeping one hand teasing my chest, I slip my shorts down and off. I trace a finger along my panties, feeling the dampness through the fabric, "Fuck, you've already got me soaked through my good-girl panties. But you already knew that, didn't you? You know exactly what you do to me."

Needing more, I slip my fingers into my panties, moving along my slit and coating myself with my juices. Circling my clit with the pads of my fingers, I sigh. "Mmm, God, that feels good. You're going to make me come rubbing my little clit like that." Rubbing in circles, I lay my head back, breathing deeply.

Closing my eyes, I let the fantasy take over completely. He makes me feel wanton, but I can't imagine saying these things if he were actually in front of me. I'd probably die of embarrassment first, and he'd definitely shut me down. But alone in my room, I feel brave, free to let loose all the dirty thoughts I have to get me to my climax.

"I need more, Professor. You stand up there, all stern and serious, lecturing us. But all I think about is that thick cock bulging in your jeans. I want to taste it, I want to take it in my virgin pussy." As I dream it's his rock-hard cock, I press two fingers inside myself, the tightness of my walls quivering against the invasion. "That's it, fill me up. I know it's a tight fit, but I can take you." I add a third finger, the stretch verging on pain, but it's so delicious, I cry out.

A constant stream of sounds, some dirty words, and some incoherent moans work their way up my throat as I slide my fingers in and out, still teasing my clit with my thumb. "Fuck, yes. Professor. I'm going to come. My sweet, untouched pussy. God, I need you to show me . . . show what I'm capable of." His earlier words rush out, no longer the encouragement of professor to student, but in my mind, they've twisted into a scenario where he works my body masterfully, taking control and teaching me things about pleasure I've never dreamed.

I stroke my clit one last time and convulsions tear through me as I whisper *Connor* over and over again, unable to do anything but ride out the wave of my orgasm. It's huge, bigger than I've ever had, and when it subsides, I find myself gasping for breath.

I peel my eyes open, thankful the couch is still holding me up because I'm complete jelly. "Holy Shit," I say to the empty room, a smile sweeping across my face. "Looks like I'm already learning some things, Professor."

I grab my drenched undies, wiping my cream-covered fingers on them. With a sigh, I decide a shower is just what I need after that workout. Both the mental one from the online chat with the professor and the physical one at my own hands.

I close my notebook, stacking it with my textbook, then close my laptop, adding it to the pile. I gently toss the whole stack onto my bed and head to the shower, promising myself that 1 will spend the weekend studying. After all, Professor Daniels said he thinks I'm capable of exceptional work, and I'm damn sure going to prove that to be true.

CHAPTER 4

CONNOR

uck. I've had women throw themselves at me before. I'm a young, good-looking, muscled-up math nerd. The idiosyncrasy of a hot-bodied intellect who can talk high-level math and superheroes is like candy to a certain type of woman. The same is true for students too. More than one young co-ed has thought she'd be the one to tempt me into breaking that taboo line, whether for grades or sport, or maybe because she was truly attracted to me. I've never once considered it. Until today.

I've already broken about a dozen rules, and probably some laws, with Daisy Phillips in my mind, but I knew I wouldn't ever act on those thoughts. But when she leaned forward, knowingly and intentionally showing her tits to me, I'd been so close to making those filthy thoughts a reality. I'd tried to let her down easy, even if my tongue did slip a bit, but I could see her humiliation.

I go back to work, grading papers at my desk. It's only moments later that I hear a rustling. At first, I think someone's in the room with me, and I scan the small space, finding myself alone as I thought. But then the noise happens again.

And then I hear it. A breathy sigh.

And Daisy's voice.

My eyes look to my computer screen, the chat window still there but showing a solid black screen. The chat is closed, right?

I click on it "Miss Phillips? Can you hear me?"

No response.

At least not to me, but what I do hear makes me instantly hard. It's Daisy, obviously masturbating, judging by the sounds. And if that wasn't enough to get me rock fucking hard instantly, when she says my name, I'm fully erect in seconds.

I try again, knowing that this is wrong. Clicking on the window, I see if she can hear me. "Daisy?"

Still no response. But her words are getting dirtier, and after a moment of hesitation, I can't help myself. If she can't hear me talking to her, trying to warn her of the continued connection, she won't hear me touching myself either. I hope that's true, because fuck, I can't help it.

As she works herself, her moans and words streaming live to my ears, I do the same, taking my cock in hand. I fuck my hand, using my precum to ease the way. It's an erotic aural assault, but in my mind, I picture her just as she was on the screen, messy hair and glasses, tits pushed up in her bra, but the image morphs, turning into her naked and writhing beneath me, and I pump myself harder and faster.

She's mid-stream of dirty talk when I hear her say 'my virgin pussy', and I have to grab the base of my cock and squeeze hard to stave off the immediate orgasm. Could she be telling the truth? Is she actually a virgin? I'd imagined that but never really believed it could be true. Inexperienced, for sure, but untouched? She's a gorgeous woman, brilliant and interesting. How has no other man popped that cherry?

The thought of anyone else tasting her sweetness, breaking through that barrier for the first time, infuriates me. Like some silly high school boy or barely old enough college frat boy is worth her gift. No, I want it. I want her first time, and maybe more after that.

The thought is delicious, a momentary imagining that while it sounds so right, I know it's so very wrong. But I let my fantasy take me away as I pump myself. And when she gets close, I pick up my pace, wanting to match her, to come with her, both of us together, even if she doesn't know it.

As she cries out, I hear her whispering my name over and over like a prayer, and I explode, ropes of white cum trickling down my hand as I ride out the forceful orgasm with her. "Daisy . . ." I grunt out.

I hear her panting breaths in time with mine as we both recover. And then, too soon, the black chat window winks out, disappearing. For an instant, I think maybe I imagined it. But then I look at my cock, and I know the truth.

I just heard Daisy Phillips rubbing her sweet pussy . . . to me. No, her sweet *virgin* pussy as she imagined me taking her.

I am so fucked. Because damn, do I want to make her dream a reality. Actually, it's my dream too.

THE WEEKEND IS WAY TOO LONG AND NOT NEARLY LONG enough. Dean Michaels called about some fundraising event he wants me to speak at and one of my doctoral candidate students called with a crisis. Both of the phone calls had only paused my obsession with Daisy. I worked out mercilessly, trying to will my body into submission through exhaustion, but every post-workout shower had me jacking off to the memory of her breathy moans and my name on her lips.

I vacillate all weekend between not saying a word to Daisy and telling her what I heard after our chat. I should probably keep it a secret, protect her pride and my reputation. And I've told myself that's the game plan, time after time.

What I want to do to her could put my career in jeopardy . . . but I almost feel like it'd be worth it. To bend her over, to turn what I'm sure is a creamy pale ass bright pink from spanking. To make her get on her knees and worship my cock, make her beg before I turn her around and pound her until I cream so deep and so hard inside her it drips out of her afterward.

No. I can't. She's off limits in so many ways. She's my student, she's so young, she's a virgin, she's so fucking sexy, she wants me. Shit. I got off track again. She's not for me, I remind myself.

I tell myself that again as I walk into the teacher's lounge for coffee, knowing that she'll be in my next class.

"Get yourself in gear," I admonish myself, reaching for my phone. "Coffee, email, grab my notes . . ."

"Yo, CD, what's up?" a familiar voice says, and I turn to see Nick Goodman, my friend and fellow professor.

"H–hey, Nick," I stammer, worrying for a second that he can read my dangerously dirty thoughts on my face. "What's up?"

"You okay?" Nick asks, coming all the way in. "Your face is all flushed. You thinking some naughty thoughts about those improper fractions again?"

It's an old joke between us, but still, I almost forget to laugh. "Ha ha, man. Seriously, get some new material."

He grins devilishly. "How about . . . what's 6.9?"

I eye him and shrug.

"Good sex interrupted by a period," he says, laughing at his own juvenile humor.

I give him a sympathy smirk. "I've got class in fifteen. What do you need?"

"Just wanted to know if you heard about Cunningham over at MIT," he asks, grinning. Rob Cunningham has been one of the leading professors in the STEM field for twenty years and someone I've admired for awhile. He's the most likely contender for the Abel Prize, basically, the Nobel Prize for mathematics, next year.

"I've been too busy. What's going on?"

"Rumor has it that he dipped his wick in the TA well," Nick says. "And there's video."

"Oh, shit," I rasp, blinking. "How'd that happen?"

"How do you think? The dumbshit probably kept the video on his phone and his wife found it," Nick says gleefully. "Man, was she pissed. I don't know if she was more or less mad that . . . the TA wasn't a girl."

"No fucking way," I reply, surprised at both Cunningham's falter and his preference. "So is she taking him to the cleaners?"

"And some . . . her family is a *big* contributor to the school, so there's word his tenure might be in jeopardy," Nick says, shaking his head. "More because of who she is than what he did, but it shakes out ugly for him either way. Anyway, just wanted you to know, since I know you've been watching his work. Might put a damper on his shoe-in win for the Abel."

"Yeah," I murmur, still disbelieving. Although I can definitely understand the temptation after this weekend. "Listen, man, no offense, but—"

"Hey, I know. I have shit to do too," Nick says. "See you later."

Heading to my office, I silently talk myself through the game plan again. It's best if I stay away from her. If that means I need to grade her more fairly . . . well, so be it. I don't like not pushing her, but maybe that'll keep her away. I don't want to end up like Cunningham, and after what I did Friday night, I know I crossed a line.

I grab my notes along with the papers I need to return and hurry to the lecture room, arriving just a minute before class. I sit down, and I quickly glance around, not seeing Daisy. *Maybe she's absent today. Maybe she—*

The door opens and she walks in. Passing right by my desk, I can smell her, and I have to force my eyes to stay on my papers as I can almost smell the soft, sexy scent of her pussy, that smooth virgin pussy, begging for me.

Goddammit. I'm going to have to do some camouflaging . . . because I'm hard as a fucking rock again. This is going to be a battle.

And I don't intend to lose.

The next hour is painstakingly slow. I can't just hide behind my desk. Everyone would wonder why I'm not up and around, engaging the class like usual. So I face the whiteboard as much as possible.

But when I see Daisy crossing and uncrossing her legs, I can barely hold back the groan. Before my brain can stop it, my mouth spits out, "Miss Phillips, perhaps you can show us how you'd solve this problem?"

She jerks in her seat, surprise showing on her face for an instant before she smiles. "Sure, Professor Daniels." She walks to the board and gets to work.

I take the opportunity to check her out under the guise of watching her scribble neat lines of equations. She's wearing a skirt today. I think the girls call them 'skater skirts', but all I know is that with one twirl, I bet it'd spin out and show me her panties underneath. Her good-girl panties. I want to flip her skirt up, slip the cotton down her thighs, and feast on her.

As if she hears my thoughts, she turns. "What do you think?"

I freeze, then my brain clicks back on and I let a slow smile take my face. "Excellent work, Miss Phillips." I point to a line in her work. "You'll notice she did a bit of multi-tasking in this line, both solving for X and reorg'ing the integers. That's fine, or you could break that out into two steps if you'd prefer."

"Oh," she says with a jump. Marker still in her hand, she approaches me and then adds a closing parenthesis to one of the lower lines. "Got it."

I dip my chin, my voice husky. "Good catch. You're learning."

Clearing my throat, I address the room. "All right, class dismissed until Wednesday. Complete problems ten through twenty-five in unit five to be prepared, as we'll be moving on to the next section."

There's a hint of a groan at the homework assignment, but I'm already out the door, rushing to my office to get some needed space before I do something supremely stupid.

CHAPTER 5

*P*rofessor Daniels basically bolts from the room after dismissing class. But after his help on Friday night—with my math work, *not* my orgasm—I feel like I should thank him again. Especially for the compliment that has reaffirmed my love affair with math once again, something I felt was in jeopardy with his harsh grading.

I knock twice on his office door, waiting until I hear his gruff permission to enter. I open the door tentatively. "Professor Daniels?"

I step in the office, closing the door behind me. I swear his eyes skate along my body, head to toe and back up to meet my eyes. It happens so fast, it could be my imagination. But there is something in his eyes as he stares at me. I can't decide if it's anger or lust, but there is definitely heat.

"Can I help you with something, Miss Phillips?" he asks, his voice tight as he leans back in his chair, crossing his arms over his chest. His biceps bulge against his black t-shirt, and I realize that instead of a little alligator on the chest, there's a pi symbol. A math joke, but the look on his face is anything but funny.

I hesitate. Maybe this isn't such a good idea. But telling him thank you can't be a bad thing, right? "No, I just wanted to say thank you again for the help Friday night."

He flinches, although I don't know why. "No problem. That's what I'm here for, to teach you." He gulps.

I'm not sure what to say. I'm used to his being this powerhouse of cocky asshole, but right now, he seems almost nervous around me. "I know. And I'm learning. I definitely am. So I just wanted to tell you how much I appreciate the extra help and the kind words about my work." My nerves are getting the better of me, my mouth rambling and my brain not stopping it. "I was getting concerned that maybe I wasn't cut out to be a math major, so hearing that you think I have potential really reassured me. I promise to show you just what I'm capable of."

He groans. He legit lets out a deep, throaty noise that makes me think of sex.

"I heard you, Daisy." He says it and then snaps his mouth shut like he hadn't meant to let the words out. I'm confused. Of course, he heard me. I just talked to him. I tilt my head questioningly.

He swallows like he wishes he could take the words back, but with a fortifying breath, he says, "I *heard* you . . . Friday night." He emphasizes the words with a lift of his eyebrows.

And suddenly, I realize what he means. "Oh, God. This cannot be happening." I shake my head, the flush already rushing to my cheeks as I bury my face in my hands.

He gets up, rushing around his desk and squatting down beside me. "It's okay, Daisy. Nothing to be embarrassed about. We all have needs and it's perfectly natural to take care of them. I don't know what happened to the chat window. I tried to tell you, but you couldn't hear me."

I lift my face, bravely meeting his eyes. "But you could hear me?"

He nods but looks off to the side. I feel in my gut that he's not being fully truthful with me.

"Could you . . . uhm, could you *see* me?" I ask, my voice soft. I'm still embarrassed, mortified, actually, but there's a heat in my core. A small part of me is turned on by his witnessing my private moment.

"No, I couldn't see you. Just a black window. I swear it." He takes my hands in his as he shakes his head.

"But you listened. You know what I was doing, heard my fantasy?" I'm not sure what I want his answer to be. The only reason I was able to say those things was because I was alone. But the humiliation of his turning down my semi-offered proposal Friday night is being replaced completely by the idea that he listened, and more importantly, that he liked what he heard.

He swallows, but I can see the smirk teasing his lips. He *did* like it. The knowledge gives me courage that I ordinarily wouldn't possess. Though his hands are holding mine in comfort, I move my palms down my thighs, slipping my skirt up higher. His hands follow my movements, not guiding me but going along for the ride wherever I take them.

"Daisy . . ." he warns, but his eyes are locked on the line where my thighs disappear under my skirt. I move up another inch.

"Do you want to see?" I ask, biting my lip hopefully. Any embarrassment I felt is gone as his hands clench mine tightly. He probably means to stop me, but I take it as encouragement. I lift my skirt the rest of the way, my white cotton panties coming into view.

"Fuck . . ." he whispers. He places his hands on my thighs, and at the slightest pressure, I spread for him. "I can already see you're soaked for me," he growls, taking a big inhale. I've never thought of my scent being anything special, but he seems to savor it like it's a treat.

I move my fingers down, rubbing along my pussy through the cotton, so much like my fantasy that I can't help but say the same things again. "You already know what you do to me. I'm soaked for you every damn day, making myself come to your arrogant grins and that cock you keep hidden in your jeans." I thought I'd be too shy to say these things to him, but his heated gaze makes me want to tell him all my filthy thoughts.

"Show me." It's not a request. It's an order. One I happily obey. I pull my panties to the side, my bare

46

mound and glistening lips coming into view, but he shakes his head. I have a second of doubt. Did I read this wrong? But then his hands are reaching up on my hips, pulling my panties down and off. He stuffs them in his back pocket and his hands go back to my thighs, spreading me even wider. "So fucking pretty, Daisy," he says reverently. "Now show me." His commanding tone is gravel-rough on my skin, the vibrations tickling and tantalizing.

I let my fingers trace through my folds, gathering my juices and slicking up to my engorged clit. He watches as I touch myself, his breathing matching my quickening pace. His gaze is hot, a palpable thing as I take myself higher and higher.

"Touch me?" I ask, but I can hear the pleading tone in my voice.

But he shakes his head. "I can't . . . I shouldn't. This is so fucking wrong." He's visibly fighting with himself, holding onto what's left of his control by a thread. I want to cut that thread, see and feel him unleashed with no holds barred.

"Just one finger, Professor Daniels? One finger in my virgin pussy so I have something to squeeze against? I'm so close. Please," I beg.

"Goddamn it, Daisy." But even as he curses me, he rewards me, giving me the single finger I so desperately need. He teases my opening. "Are you really a virgin?"

I bite my lip and nod, his acquiescence driving me to the edge of craziness.

"This sweet little pussy has never been fucked hard and filled with cum?" I moan at his words, and then again as he slowly slips his thick finger inside. I feel every inch as he fills me and retreats to do it again, maddeningly slow.

I rub my clit faster, on the edge from the feeling of any part of him inside me. I manage to gasp out, "I'm coming, Professor."

He leans forward and growls in my ear, finger deep in my pussy. "Daisy, you had no problem calling me Connor when you came to a fantasy of me. Call me by my name when you come for me now."

"Yes, Connor. Fuck!" I don't close my eyes, needing to see him to believe this is real as I come hard. My body bows up, searching for every bit of pleasure he'll give me, and the waves crash and crash over me, one after another. I'm panting when I see him slip his finger from me, the loss instant and significant. But when he lifts his finger to his mouth and sucks my juices, savoring them the way he did my scent, I'm struck with a thought.

"Now you," I say, not a question.

"What?" he asks, still seemingly lost in the moment.

"When you listened to me, did you touch yourself? Did you jack off your big cock as you heard me calling out your name?" I can tell by his grin that he did.

"And what if I did?" The words are a challenge, a dare if ever I heard one.

"Show me."

I can see the argument formulating in his mind, the

words on the tip of his tongue. But he squashes them. In for an ounce, in for a pound, I guess. "You sure you can handle this?" He's still challenging me, the words so similar to the last time I was in his office and freaked out over some innuendo.

But I'm not freaking this time. No way, no how. Look at me, a fucking vixen I never would've suspected I was capable of being. But he brings it out in me, like so many other things. I bite my lip and nod, encouraging him.

He stands, resting back against his desk, and his hard cock pressing against his jeans comes into view. My eyes flicker to it, my mouth instantly watering. Jesus, I've never even touched a dick before . . . but all I can think of right now is swallowing every inch of what he's got.

His deft fingers unbuckle his belt, then he undoes the button and zipper, slipping his jeans down his hips a bit. His cock is pulsing beneath the fabric of his black boxer briefs. And then he lowers them, his cock coming into view.

"You're . . . beautiful," I whisper, taking in his cock. Maybe that's not the conventional word for a man's dick, but he is. Smooth and thick, with a vein pulsing along each side of his length and a round head that's already leaking fluid.

He wraps his hand around the shaft, pumping himself a few times. "Is this what you want to see?" he says. His voice almost sounds . . . angry? I tear my eyes away from the sexy show he's putting on to look up to his face. He looks tortured, like this is hurting him.

"Are you okay?" I ask, concerned and confused. I thought guys liked this and did this all the time, so why does he seem furious?

"No, it's not fucking okay, Daisy. You're my student, I'm your professor, and this is wrong. But I can't stop. You're . . . so fucking sexy, and I want your eyes on me, watching what you do me the way I just watched what I do to you." The words are stilted, in time with the thrust of his hips as he fucks his hand.

My heart rate speeds up. He's not in pain. He's fighting himself, fighting this over some sense of right and wrong. But I want this. So fucking badly.

I grab his thighs where they're spread in front of me. "Let me. Teach me." I don't wait for him to answer. I just wrap my hands around his. My first touch of cock is . . . warm and silky soft. I try to wrap my fingers around him and fail, not able to hold him completely in one hand. The tip is beautiful, flared and wide, making me marvel at how it could fit inside me . . . and what that ridge would do as it plowed in and out of my pussy.

I lick my lips, letting my hand caress down to his balls, huge and heavy. I look back up at him, almost pleading for him to guide me because I don't know what I'm doing.

He switches our position, laying his hands over mine and showing me how to stroke him. Once I have the hang of it, he lets go to let me be in control of the pace. His hands go to the edge of the desk behind him, gripping hard as he throws his head back in pleasure, groaning quietly.

A drop of precum pearls on his tip, and I'm struck with the need to taste him. I stick my tongue out, lapping at him like a kitten, his flavor bursting across my tongue, and I moan in delight.

"Fuck, Daisy. You don't have to. Your hands on me feel so good."

I want more of those noises, guttural vibrations that make my pussy quiver in need. And so I lean forward in the chair to take him in my mouth, letting him stretch my lips wide as I suck his tip and swirl my tongue around, hoping for more of his precum. He lets me explore for a bit and then takes control.

I moan as Connor starts fucking my face slowly, pumping in and out of my eager lips. He's so much that each time his cock hits the back of my throat, I feel like I'm going to gag, but I don't care. I want . . . I want to be his naughty student, and I suck as eagerly as I can, worshipping his pulsating manhood as he looks down into my eyes. "That's it," he says as I run my tongue around his shaft. "That's a good girl. See if you can take it all for me."

His hips speed up, my pussy clenching around the ghost of what I want as his cock swells, and I moan again around him. "Now!" Connor growls, thrusting hard in my mouth. I feel the head of his cock slip into my throat before it swells, and suddenly, he's coming, pulling back slightly to fill my mouth with his sweet and salty cream. I moan again deeply, my thighs quivering as he empties himself into my mouth.

When he's done, he looks down, smiling. "Fuck, Daisy. That was . . . fuck."

It might be the best compliment he's ever given me. The thought that I can reduce such a brilliant mind to babbling is a powerful boost to my first-timer's nerves.

He tucks himself back into his boxers and jeans and then pulls me to standing. I realize this is the first time I've ever stood this close to him, body to body, sharing the same space. He towers over me by several inches, and when he wraps his arms around me, I feel safe in the cocoon of his presence.

And then he kisses me. I know he can probably taste himself on my tongue, but he doesn't seem to mind as he demands entry. It's a kiss of promise, that this isn't over, that we're not done.

But the spell is broken when I hear a soft *ding*. He breaks apart, pressing his forehead to mine as he cups my face. "I have to go. That's my ten-minute warning for my next class. And I don't think it'll look good if I go in with a hard-on."

I grin, sassing back. "Actually, I prefer class when you're hard. Makes the math that much more challenging because I'm distracted. I'll be even more distracted now."

He swats my ass over my skirt. "Cheeky brat. It's usually not a problem, except when I have a sexy student in my front row, chewing on her pencils as she studies me as much as the math."

I grin, letting my hand dip down to trace his soft length

in his jeans. "Oh, I'm studying, all right. Have a good class, Professor."

And with a laugh, I open the door, realizing it'd been unlocked the whole time. Shit, that could've been bad if we'd been caught. Luck must be on our side, though, because we weren't disturbed at all. It's not until I'm walking down the hallway that I feel a slight breeze on my pussy and realize he kept my panties. I almost turn back to retrieve them but decide I'd rather he kept them.

CHAPTER 6

*T*hat was the hottest thing I've ever done. From the way she looked, eagerly taking me in her mouth, to the way she wrapped her hand around my cock in wonder, almost worshipping it before I pumped in and out of her hungry mouth. Fuck, if we had time, I would've loved to watch her rub herself with my cock in her mouth. Talk about fucking hot.

And she took instruction well, not surprisingly, considering how quick she catches on in class. I grin to myself. Class. It seems I might be instructing Daisy in two subjects soon. One can dream.

Still, as I head to the break room, wanting to grab a better coffee than what my poor office machine can provide, I can't help but worry. We didn't just cross a line. We obliterated that motherfucker and left it so far in the dust that I can't ever go back. I'm risking getting fired, losing my reputation, losing everything I've busted my ass for.

Worst of all, I couldn't help myself. Daisy creates such a deep need in me that I would have done nearly anything to have her like that. That's dangerous, because now that I've had a taste . . . there's no way it ends here. No way I'm going to quit while I'm ahead. That pussy is mine.

As my students arrive and I start going into the nuances of Cauchy-Riemann equations, I can't help but think about Daisy. My mind wavers back and forth between what I want and what is proper.

I really should tell her we can't continue this. It's too dangerous, and I can't take the risk. Still, every time I think of even her name, I'm spellbound by the image of her wet pussy pressed up against those sheer white panties and the thought that she has never felt a man inside her yet . . . and I could be the first.

It's a miracle that I make it through my presentation and dismiss the class.

By Wednesday's class, I'm desperate to see her again even as the battle between my brain and my cock rages on. So far, my greedy desire is winning hands-down.

Daisy walks in, head held high, in another skirt paired with a V-neck T-shirt that shows her cleavage off delightfully. She looks casual but sexy as fuck. She spins a bit as she sits, her skirt flaring to flash an enticing hint of upper thigh. Her eyes snap to mine, making sure I saw her show, and there's a moment of freeze, where I'm holding my body in place by force, fighting against the urge to kiss her hello. That would be the kiss of death to my career, and we both know it.

She smirks a bit, knowing what her outfit and her sass do to me. Bratty girl needs a lesson. And I'm just the teacher to give her one.

The class is painfully slow, torture for us both as I loom near her desk in the middle of the front row. But I don't make eye contact with her. That'd let her win this round. Instead, I keep my eyes scanning the room, calling on everyone except her, but I can feel her attention on me the whole time. I feel the heat of her gaze on my ass and on my crotch when I turn to face each side of the room. I sense her crossing and uncrossing her legs as I drive her crazy, teasing her with what she wants and knowing she can't have in the middle of class.

By the time the clock ticks the hour past, my lesson for her benefit is having its own consequences for me. I'm glad my boxer briefs and jeans are holding me tight or else class would've been rather obscene. But I'm uncomfortable in the pinched confines, and she needs to pay for that too.

"Okay, class, until Friday. Complete the next unit's homework problems, paying particular attention to the format for your answers. Dismissed." I wait a beat, letting the din of everyone packing up and rushing for the door fill the room, then speak again, harsh and unforgiving. "Miss Phillips, I'd like to speak with you about your homework, if you have a moment?"

Her eyes are wide as saucers, fear sparking in their depths, but she nods.

I sit on my desk, letting my feet dangle as the room empties.

I see Daisy's seatmate, Sabrina, lean toward her. She stage-whispers, "Good luck, Daisy. Do you want me to wait for you?"

Daisy offers her a smile. "Thanks, but it's okay. I swear I was extra-precise with the homework. It can't be all bad." Sabrina nods but obviously doesn't agree, firmly in the camp that believes I'm a math monster that eats students' GPAs for breakfast.

Right now, I'm thinking there's something else I'd rather eat . . . Daisy's sweet little pussy. But I have class in this very room in fifteen minutes, so there's no time for what I want to do to her. Time. I need time.

Finally alone, she approaches the desk, standing between my spread legs, but far enough away that it'd seem appropriate to anyone who peeked in the room. "Yes, sir? My homework?" she says, but the lift of her eyebrow says she knows I didn't keep her here to talk about the *A* she got on the last set of problems I assigned.

Keeping the double-talk going, I ask, "How were you feeling after Monday's *work*? Any concerns, problems we need to go over?"

She digs the toe of her shoe into the floor, looking down and every inch the innocent that she is, but then she remembers herself and stands tall and proud. The reminder of how inexperienced she is sets me afire, and I grip the edge of the desk to stop from touching her.

"No, I felt good . . . really good about the work. Ready to learn more, in fact." She smiles, an invitation in her eyes.

"Another tutoring session then? You really are capable of such exceptional work. You're just raw and untrained. I'm happy to mentor you." I'm offering more, so much more than math help, or hell, even sexual guidance, but I don't know how to broach the breadth and depth of what I want with her in this class-room where we could be overheard.

"Yes, Professor Daniels. That'd be great. I appreciate your help," she says, her voice dripping sex.

I grab a Post-It note from my desk, scribbling my address down. "Meet me here at seven tonight and we'll make sure the previous lesson stuck. We'll build from there."

She steps forward to take the paper from my hand, the electricity shooting between us at the barest touch. She clutches it to her chest. "Yes, sir. Seven tonight for tutoring."

She moves to step away, and I can't bear to let her go without more. I hop from the desk, grabbing her upper arm to stop her. "Oh, and Daisy?"

She looks at me expectantly, and I do a quick sweep of the doorway, making sure no students are entering.

Seeing no one, I slip my hand under her skirt, pinching her ass sharply. She gasps, but as I soothe the sting with a brush of my palm, she moans quietly. I whisper harshly into her ear, "Don't flash what's mine to anyone else. You'd best take care when you wear skirts like this or I'll have to spank your bratty ass for showing off to anyone but me. Understood?"

She nods silently. I smooth the fabric down over her ass, making sure it's as long as possible and hiding the treasure of her pussy from every other fucker on campus. Stepping back, I give her a raised eyebrow and a smirk, knowing that she's already wet for me. It feels like a win, even though I'm equally anxious for tonight.

By seven, I'm not rock-hard anymore. I'm a fucking steel rod, ready to claim her virginity like the cocky bastard I am. The doorbell rings, and I open it to see Daisy wearing the skirt from earlier. I grin, ready to flip it up and fill her.

But I force myself to have some manners. "Come in."

She steps in nervously, looking around like my space is going to give her insight into who I am. Actually, that might be true, I think, as I glance to the living room, seeing through her eyes. A comfy leather couch claims most of the room, surrounded with a big screen television and bookcases full of a mix of textbooks and comics. It looks like what it is . . . a bachelor's pad. Mostly function, not form.

She wrings her hands together, stammering. "I took the

bus from school so no one would see my car nearby. I didn't want to cause any problems by being here."

She's smart, so fucking smart. I honestly hadn't even thought of that, my mind too tangled up in thoughts of her spread wide before me to worry about how it would look to have a student's car sitting in my driveway. It's not likely anyone whould notice, but it's still a senseless risk. "Good thinking." She preens at the simple praise.

"Want something to eat? I made dinner, nothing fancy but it's edible," I say, leading her into the kitchen. She looks around again, the small table set for two with simple plates and silverware.

"You made me dinner?" she asks, obviously surprised. She's so easily pleased by the simplest of gestures. I wonder if she thought I was just going to attack her when she walked through the door. Admittedly, it did occur to me, but I want her first time to be special, to set the tone for more for us.

I spoon the noodles on the plates as I gesture for her to sit down. Her skirt flares only slightly as she sits, proof that her move in class was intentional. The thought of her trying to seduce me turns me on. As if she needs to do anything more than simply be her beautiful, brilliant self. "Just pasta and jarred sauce. The bread was already garlic-coated too. I'm not really much of a cook, but a date requires food, typically, so I did my best."

She smiles wide. "Is that what this is? A date?"

I realize with a start that she has no idea at the thoughts rolling through my head. No experience with which to compare. She probably thinks this is some casual fuck for me, just a notch in my bedpost of co-eds I've done this with a hundred times before.

It's not. *She's* not.

I sit across from her, urging her to eat. "Daisy, I don't want to mince words here or talk in veiled innuendo like earlier. I want you to be honest with me." It's not a question, but she nods anyway. "I don't fuck students. Ever. It's unprofessional and could have dire consequences for me."

She swallows the mouthful of spaghetti, wiping at her lips with her napkin. "But I thought—"

I interrupt her. "You thought you were coming here tonight for me to fuck you?" She nods, her eyes shining with confusion. "And God help me, I want to fuck you, pop your sweet cherry and claim your pussy as mine. But . . ." I pause, making sure her eyes are focused on me. "But I am not willing to do that casually. If I wanted a casual fuck, I could have one of dozens. If I'm risking everything here, it's only if it's *more*."

Her smile dawns slowly as my words hit home, their meaning resonating in the space between us. "More. I like the sound of more." She sighs, impossibly more beautiful, as she commits to something she doesn't fully understand. But I do. And isn't that the point? I'll teach her.

I stand, leaving my barely-touched dinner. I'm not hungry for food. I'm hungry for her. Her pure innocence. Her sassy mouth. Her sexy body. Her brilliant mind. Her sweet spirit. All of her. All mine.

Taking her hand, I guide her to stand, cupping her chin in my other hand. "Are you sure, Daisy? There are no second chances here. No do-overs or retakes. Choose carefully." My voice is hard, brooking no argument, demanding that she think before speaking.

After staring into my eyes, searching for something she must find, she speaks. "I'm sure. Make love to me, Connor."

I smirk. "Oh, honey, I'm not going to make love to you. I'm going to fuck you raw and hard until you fall apart for me, my name the only thing on your lips. But I will fuck you with all my heart, Daisy." I want her to hear the difference. This won't be some soft, romantic moment like her teenage self dreamed about. I'm going to claim her, ruin her for any other man but me, but it won't matter because my cock is the only one her pussy is ever going to get.

I lead her down the hallway to my bedroom. The bedside lamp is on, but she doesn't scan this room like the others. No, her eyes stay locked on me, waiting for my lead, my direction.

I guide her to stand beside the bed, dropping to my knees to slip her shoes off. Tossing them aside, I run my hands up her legs, feeling the taut muscle beneath the silk of her skin. Up under her skirt, I cup her ass, kneading her flesh in my large palms. She whimpers, her hands shooting to my shoulders to hold herself steady as she rocks into my hands.

"You're wet for me, aren't you? I can smell you from here, sweet like candy, begging me to lick you all up." I pull her panties down and off, laying them neatly on my bedside table.

She grins down at me. "If you keep taking my panties, I'm not going to have any left to wear. You want me walking around campus naked beneath my skirts where anyone could see my pussy if the wind blew just right?"

Her bratty challenge reminds me of her behavior in class today. I rise, crowding her against the bed, but to her credit, she doesn't fall backward. Instead, she presses her body against mine. "You'll wear panties at all times unless I tell you otherwise, Daisy. No one sees this pussy but me. No one touches it but me. That includes you. You don't touch yourself unless I say so. I'll give you all the pleasure you could ever need. Understood?"

"Yes, sir," she says, her sass spurring me on.

"Turn around and bend over the bed." She lifts an eyebrow but obeys. I flip her skirt up, exposing her round cheeks to my eyes. I can see her slick pussy, so needy already. I cup her ass in my hands, squeezing the flesh roughly. "I'd considered taking it easy on you, postponing the punishment for your behavior in class today or maybe letting you off this one time since you're still learning, after all. But something tells me by the way you're still pushing me that you don't want me to let you skate by. You want this, don't you?" I ask her, but I already know the answer. And when she looks back at me, mouth open in anticipation as she gasps, she knows that I've already figured her out. I grin ferally at her, letting her see the animal she's provoked.

I rear back and deliver a sharp smack to her right cheek.

She jolts forward and cries out, but before the pain even registers, I'm already soothing her pinkened skin. "That's for teasing me in class, knowing full fucking well that you were *this close* to showing off that pussy to every fucker in the room." Her hips roll under my hands, begging for more. Not one to disappoint, I smack her left cheek, the sound echoing in the room. I immediately trace my palm there again, taking away the sting. "And that one's for the bratty sass that you know drives me insane, but I think that's why you do it, isn't it, honey?"

Daisy groans into the comforter, hips bucking and her honey spreading down her thighs. I spread her cheeks, wanting a closer look at her pink center. "Fuck, Daisy. Know what you get when you take your punishment like a good girl?" My breath is hot on her pussy, her intoxicating scent invading my pores, filling me with longing.

"What? What do good girls get?" she breathes out, her voice tight with eagerness.

Though I use my mouth, I don't answer in words. My tongue laps at her cream, tasting her cotton-candy sweetness right from the source. She cries out, instinctively spreading her legs to let me have better access. I moan against her, knowing the vibration will spread to her clit. I follow the tremor and swirl my tongue against her button, circling over and over.

"Oh, my God, Connor. I didn't know it could feel like that. Fuck, so good." Her cries are music to my ears as her body shudders against me.

I slip a finger in her pussy, fucking her slow and shallow to test how tight she is. She damn-near choked my fingers at the slightest invasion before, and I know my cock is going to be in tortured heaven inside her. But I need to get her ready or I'll never get inside without hurting her.

She relaxes, pressing back against me, seeking more. "Yes, honey. That's it. Take it and come on my hand and my mouth." She does as instructed, working herself enough that I'm able to add a second finger, and then a third, though it's a tight fit and I know it has to be bordering on pain for her. "Good girl, Daisy. Let me in so I can get you ready for me."

The thought of my filling her with my cock triggers her, and she bucks wildly, coming instantly. The gush of her cream eases the way, and my three fingers slip in and out easily as I push her higher and longer, wanting every drop of pleasure for her.

She collapses forward, the bed and my arm wrapped around her middle holding her up. I slip my fingers from her pussy and straight into my mouth, wanting more of her taste on my tongue. I could eat her out every day and still want more.

I pull her to stand, spinning her in my arms and covering her mouth with a kiss. She's gasping by the time I let her breathe. "Are you done, Daisy? Or can you take more?"

Her wicked grin tells me the answer even before she speaks. "More, please, Professor." The return to calling me 'professor' during such a sexy moment should turn me off, but instead, it riles me up, playing up the taboo of what we're doing.

"Okay, if you want it like that, Miss Phillips," I say, emphasizing her formal name, "let's see if you can follow directions to the letter for once." It's a mild admonishment, but she rises to the challenge, ever competitive and willing to do her best.

"Take off your clothes." I step back to give her just enough space to follow the command, and I watch as she pulls the skirt down, then slips her T-shirt over her head. She pauses for a heartbeat as she reaches back to unclasp her bra, but when she sees my reprimanding look, she undoes it and tosses it aside.

She stands before me, fully nude and absolutely stunning. I want to trace every inch of her body with my tongue, memorize her every dip and curve with my hands, measure just how much she can physically take underneath me.

I yank the comforter back, wanting her in my bed. "Lie down for me." She smiles softly and climbs to the middle of the bed. Her dark hair spreads against the pillow in a halo, her tan skin contrasting starkly against the white sheets. She looks like an angel.

She writhes against the fabric, stretching her body out and extending her arms wide. "Satin sheets? Do you always sleep on satin or did you do this for tonight?"

I consider telling her a lie but decide if I want her truth, I need to give her my own. "I usually sleep and fuck on satin. It makes it easy to move and position you where I want you, and the slip of it against your skin is decadent. Do you like it?"

She nods and reaches for me, but I hold back to undress.

I yank my shirt over my head, and when I reach for my belt, I realize she's sitting up, watching me with rapt attention. I slowly slide the leather through, torturing us both with the delay but loving the way her breathing picks up. I can see her pulse thrumming in her neck, racing with excitement. My belt undone, I make quicker work of the rest and then I'm standing before her naked.

I've never felt more vulnerable. I'm in good shape and certainly not old by any standard, but I'm damn-near ten years older than Daisy, who's likely only paid attention to the shirtless college boys in the gym. I let the fire I feel for her shine in my eyes, daring her to find me lacking in any way. We stare at each other for a moment, and then the tension breaks as she breathes, "Please, Connor."

She looks at me, worried for a second, but the look in my eyes assures her as I climb in next to her. There's a bit of fear in her eyes as I position myself between her legs, but my cock is ready to take care of her as she gives me a trusting look.

Slowly, I lower down to her, covering her with my body and pressing her to the bed to grind against her, not entering her yet but teasing at the motion. She feels silkier than the satin sheets against my skin, so smooth. "Fuck, Daisy. I need you. Let me in. I need you to say it, honey."

She bites her lip, but the words come easily. "Fuck me, Connor. I want you to be my first."

I press up on one hand, the other going to my shaft to guide my way to her entrance. I need to go slow, give her an inch at a time so I don't hurt her. I breathe deeply to fortify my resolve, the urge to slam balls-deep in one stroke riding me hard.

Instead of words, I lean down, kissing her tenderly to encourage her to relax, letting my lips and my body language tell her that it's all going to be okay. Slowly, in sweet, exquisite torture, I stretch her out, working my cock in and out in short, gentle strokes.

It's amazing, sinking myself into Daisy's body, becoming one with her.

I'm barely in when her breath catches and her eyes shoot wide. "That's it, Daisy. I'm right there. Take a big breath for me, and when you exhale, there'll be a small pinch. But I swear, I'll be easy."

She nods, her trust a beautiful thing. And when she exhales, I push forward. Her breath turns into a cry, but I catch it in a kiss, holding still deep inside her. She whimpers, and I give her a few small thrusts, testing to see when she relaxes. "You okay?"

Her hips buck in response. "No, I need you to move. Fuck . . . move, please." So I do, watching her closely and feeling more like the student than the teacher in this moment. She may be learning about sex, but I'm learning her. What she likes, what makes her cry out, and what makes her tight pussy clamp down on me like a vise.

Slowly, we build the pace, finding our rhythm. She's taking me fully, long thrusts from her entrance to deep inside where I bottom out, pushing a cry of pleasure from her lips with every stroke. Our hips smack together, making Daisy gasp. "Fuck! Oh, my God, yes!"

Her encouragement drives me, and I start fucking her deeply. Hard strokes are ended each time with my hips grinding against hers, her clit rubbing against my body and making her groan. She starts calling out my name again and again with each thrust, and I have to pull out before I can't take it anymore.

"Please . . . fuck, Connor, fuck me," Daisy begs, her eyes huge and soulful. "I need you . . . so close."

I dip in again, pressing her hips to the satin to pound her almost savagely, our bodies shaking my entire bed as she clenches me. Her pussy is so tight and warm that I have to freeze again and again, torturing the both of us, but I can't help myself. If I keep going, I'm going to explode inside her . . . and I don't want this to ever end.

Daisy gasps as I freeze again, her eyes staring into my very fucking soul. Somehow, this little virgin has flipped our positions. I'm in charge . . . but she has all the power, bewitching me with her magical body and perfect, tight pussy. "Just a little more. I want to come so badly."

"That's it, little angel," I encourage, pulling back for a final sprint. "Come all over my cock! Milk my cream out of me."

With long, almost blurringly fast thrusts, Daisy and I catapult ourselves toward the onrushing precipice. My cock swells, and she cries out, my name sweet in my ears as her fingernails dig into my shoulders and she comes, squeezing me so tightly that I can't hold back any longer.

Growling her name, I explode, my cream filling her. I groan, my back arching as she clings to me, wrapping her legs around me.

I collapse onto her, wrung out and weak from everything I gave her. I bury my face into her neck, laying an open-mouthed kiss there before moving up. "Now . . . now, you're mine," I promise her, tugging on her ear with my teeth.

CHAPTER 7

DAISY

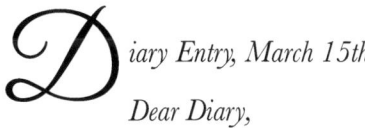 *iary Entry, March 15th*

Dear Diary,

I can't believe it! I finally did it! And it was beautiful and special and powerful. All the things I thought it would be.

I won't say who it was, even in these private pages, because it could definitely get me, and him, into trouble if anyone found out. We definitely shouldn't, but I can't help myself with him. And apparently, the feeling is mutual.

It happened so fast too. Well, not the actual event. That took all night. But before that. One minute, I thought he hated me, or at the least was annoyed by me. And then, whip-fast, I find out that maybe hate and love are closer cousins than I imagined. A few days ago, I wrote how mortified I was that I was overheard online, but now I'm thinking that was the awkward start to something really amazing.

He says I'm his. Actually, he growled 'mine' while he bit my ear, and it was unbelievably hot. And he says this is 'more', not casual.

It's hard to trust that, but fuck, do I want to. I want to believe every filthy word and promise from his mouth.

Because I do want more. And I want to be his.

BY FRIDAY'S CLASS, I'M WORKED UP BEYOND BELIEF. Connor and I had phone sex last night, another first for me. He'd guided me through touching myself the way he wanted me to, his deep voice rumbling in my head-phones as he watched me come for him. Though I didn't tell him what to do, I watched his movements, memorizing how he likes to be touched, ever his student and always wanting to learn.

But now, only hours later, I'm needy again. But there's no time, considering class starts in minutes. I consider stopping by his office, but that's a dangerous taunt of fate, so I force myself to sit in my chair and wait patiently.

"Hey, Daisy, how're you doing?" Sabrina says from beside me. Her usually bubbly voice is flat and I look over to her.

"I'm fine, but girl . . . are *you* okay? No offense, but you look a bit . . . under the weather?" I'm trying to be polite, but she looks like shit. Definitely stressed, and not her usual perky self.

She pats her hair in a vain attempt to tame the flyaways of blonde that have escaped her messy bun. The mere fact that she's got a tangle of hair on top of her head is a giveaway that something's wrong. While Sabrina isn't usually one of the overtly sexy dressers in Professor Daniels's class, she's usually pretty put-together, definitely not one of the sweats and Uggs girls. But today . . . I look down, and yep, she's wearing leggings. Although, paired with a slim-fit crop top and cardigan, she looks more casually sexy than 'just rolled out of bed'.

"I'm just having a hard time with this class and I need this grade or my scholarship is in jeopardy." As she says it, I can almost see the tears glistening in her eyes. "Are you doing better?"

I nod, cautiously telling her, "Yeah, unit four was the one that really bombed me out. Five was better. That was the *B* I got. But my quiz and homework for unit six have all been *A*s, so I think it'll balance out in the long run over the semester."

"Damn, I wish I could say the same. I'm still barely passing with a *C*-minus. I swear, I spend more time on this one class than I do all my other ones combined. Between lecture, the online class forum, and study group, you'd think it'd be smooth sailing. But I just can't get it," she says fatalistically.

"Maybe you should check with Professor Daniels about getting some help?" The words leave my mouth before I think them through. Fuck. I don't want Sabrina sitting alone in Connor's office with him. A flash of jealousy, sour and hot, shoots through me. "Or maybe there's another study group you could try?"

"Maybe. It's just so frustrating. I've always been decent at math—not great, but passable. You were right, though. Daniels is such a hardass about grading." She huffs a sigh, the annoyance loud and clear.

I cringe. I did call him that . . . and worse. But things have changed now. I understand why he's so persnickety about grading, and while it doesn't make it easier, it at least makes me less prickly about it. Trying to explain that without telling too much seems dangerous though. "He is hard, but I think he's doing it with our best interests in mind. I'll say that after bitching about losing points on the quiz over two versus three decimal points, I've been much more careful about details. And my grades have reflected that."

"You're defending him now?" Sabrina asks incredulously. "You've been one of the folks bitching with me about him all semester. Traitor."

She says it jokingly, a small smile on her lips, but it doesn't reach her eyes. She's too far gone in her pity party to really laugh at anything. But the word rings in my head like a gong. She's right. I have been mouthy about Professor Daniels's class, but after some tutoring of a different sort, I do feel more forgiving for his harsh teaching style. Hell, I like it a lot in other areas.

I wonder for a moment if I'm being too easily swayed, but when I really think about the conversations we've had and how his intent is to draw the best out of me because he sees my potential, I know that he's not in the wrong. My earlier, whiny self was mid-pity party too, and I wasn't taking personal responsibility for my own lack of care with the work. It wasn't him. It was me, and he was calling me out appropriately.

I smile gently as I try to placate Sabrina. "No, I'm not a traitor. His grading is tough, no doubt. I'm just saying that as much as I complained about it, he was right. And while it was a painful moment to see those low grades, especially the *C*, it did teach me exactly what it was supposed to." She rolls her eyes, not wanting to hear it. "What is he counting off for on your work? Are you getting the wrong answer or is it a point here and there for mistakes in your work?"

She pulls out her latest homework, with a glaring red *D* on the top, and hands it over. That is definitely one *D* I never want from Professor Daniels. I scan the page, looking for where she's losing points. "Oh, okay . . . well, this one is easy. See right here? You've got the formula wrong in your initial setup, and it seems like that was a mistake you made across the board, so it affected all your problems. Your process is sound. It was your setup. Relearn that correctly, and this unit will be a breeze for you." I emphasize the statement with a snap of my fingers and Sabrina smiles a bit wider now.

"Really? If I do that, I still have time to get a good grade on the test and that could save me. Thanks, Daisy." She seems a bit more settled now, definitely lighter, and I think I actually helped her.

Thank goodness, because here comes Professor Daniels. He walks into class looking good enough to eat, I think with a smirk. He's wearing a Comicon shirt, and my earlier consideration of him as a fanboy has significantly more merit now that I've seen the rows of comic books on his shelves at home. His jeans are light-wash, barely blue, and they look soft, making me want to caress his thighs to test my theory.

He doesn't look at me, not at all. His eyes scan the room instead. "Good morning. We've got a lot to cover and not much time, so let's get to work." He takes one last sip of his coffee before setting it on the desk, and then he turns to the board.

The next hour is a whirlwind. I don't have time to notice that he never looks at me, doesn't call on me once, and basically ignores my very existence. Okay, so maybe I do notice. But as I focus on the work he's demonstrating, I try to let the worry about that go. It's not like he can give me sex eyes in the middle of class. That'd be too obvious and get both of us into trouble. And the new formula he's showing us takes all my attention anyway.

By the end of class, my head is spinning but my brain is buzzing with the excitement of learning something totally new. Plus, the fact that Connor is intelligent enough to not just understand something so complex, but can break it down and actually teach it well, is sexy as fuck. I'm not one of those women who doesn't care if a guy can carry on a conversation as long as he's good-looking. No, I need the brains because they're the sexiest part of a man. Luckily for me, Connor has both brains and beauty. The full fucking package. Oh, and his package . . . definitely a plus.

When he dismisses us, I pack up my things slowly, intending to be the last person in class, hoping I can tempt him into doing something about the fire he's built in my brain and body. But I watch with bated breath as I see Sabrina approach him. I shamelessly eavesdrop while I pretend to check over my notes.

"Professor?" Sabrina asks him. She looks confused again, so maybe today's lesson wasn't as exciting for her as it was for me.

"Yes, Miss Bowen?" Professor says.

She stammers a bit, twirling a loose curl around her finger and looking up at him through her lashes. If I didn't know better, I'd swear she was flirting. The thought makes my stomach tighten. "I'm having some problems with some of the work and I wondered if you might have any suggestions for me."

She bites her lip, legitimately looking like the epitome of sexy innocent as she flirts with my man right in front of me. I growl inside, even though she doesn't know he's my man. He is our professor. Doesn't she have morals? You don't flirt for grades. That's like Feminism 101. Okay, so *I'm* fucking him, but it's not for grades.

It's because I . . . he . . . we . . . ugh, not going there. I can't win that argument and it's way too soon to consider this anything more than fucking, even if he did call me *his* in that growly rumble that turns me on.

Connor's eyes flick to me, and I realize that maybe my jealous growl wasn't inside as much as out loud. Shit.

"Miss Bowen, perhaps we should continue this discussion about your grades and work in private. Do you have a moment to come to my office?" His voice is neutral, bored almost, and though I'm glad he doesn't seem to be feeling Sabrina, he doesn't seem particularly impressed with me right now either.

"Of course, sir. Thanks for taking the time to help me." Her voice is breathy, almost like she just got done running or fucking. She turns to grab her bag from the seat beside me and gives me a look of sheer delight, even flashing a discreet thumbs-up.

Connor holds the door for Sabrina and then turns back to me. "Miss Phillips, did you need something?" I shake my head, not able to say what I need with Sabrina listening, but my eyes bore into his, willing him to understand. "Have a good weekend then. See you Monday."

As they walk out, I can hear Sabrina chattering. Though not her exact words, she might as well be effusing about his '*big brain*' and how '*hard she's willing to work*' for him. She's so obviously flirting with him, testing angles to see which elicit a response from him. Little does she know, the main response she's about to get is from me, the jealous girlfriend.

Is that what I am, though?

Realizing that what I'm about to do is the height of immaturity, bordering on a stage-five clinger action, I follow them down the hallway. His door is closed, so I sit in one of the chairs around the corner. I can't hear through the walls and door, but I strain to listen anyway.

It's damn-near thirty minutes later when the door creaks open. I bury my face in my laptop, clicking away as though thoroughly invested in whatever I'm working on. Truth is, it's a paper for a class that's already finished, so

I won't save whatever changes I'm making right now, but it makes a decent cover story.

From above, I hear a voice say my name. "Daisy?"

I look up to see Sabrina, smiling and bubbly once again. "Hey, Sabrina. Feeling better about class now?" The words come out with a hint of snark to them, but she doesn't seem to notice.

"Oh, yeah. Professor Daniels was great at going over everything with me. I might be all good now." She bends down, stuffing her cardigan into her bag, and when she stands, I realize exactly how tight her leggings are and how short her crop top is. While not inappropriate per se, it leaves nothing to the imagination, and the slip of midriff that shows every time she moves draws the eye like a beacon. She was in Connor's office dressed like that, flirting with him. I know it deep in my gut, and suddenly, her innocent words seem more like veiled innuendo. After all, I've been there, done that.

"Good, I'm glad," I say crisply.

She eyes me curiously. "What are you working on?"

I flash the screen at her, glad to have a ready excuse. "A paper. It's due this afternoon so I wanted to go over it one last time."

"Oh, okay. Well, I'll let you get back to it then. Thanks again for the help before class. I think I'm going to be okay." She waves two sets of matching crossed fingers. "Wish me luck! See ya Monday."

I wait for her to exit the door at the end of the hallway, counting my breaths until I can safely go into Connor's office without witnesses—thirty-one, thirty-two, thirty-three—and I get up, shoving my laptop into my bag and tossing it over my shoulder.

I stand in his open doorway, silently demanding his attention. A heartbeat later, he looks up, cocky smirk on his face as he sits back in his chair and crosses his arms over his chest. "Miss Phillips, come in. Something I can help you with?"

I enter and force myself to close the door gently, even though I want to slam the shit out of it. I drop my bag to the floor, hands on his desk in an attempt to loom over him. "What the fuck was that?" My voice is high, fury in every syllable.

Connor narrows his eyes, tiny crinkles popping at the corners as he glares at me. "That? That was me helping a student with her work. Is that a problem?"

"Ugh." I try to put every bit of the exasperation I feel into the sound. "Yes, it's a problem. Sabrina was practically throwing herself at you. What am I supposed to do with that?" I demand.

A sly grin breaks across his face before he chuckles. "You're jealous." It's not a question so I don't answer. He leans forward in his chair, putting his hands on his desk. "Sit down, Daisy."

I want to stay standing just to be contrary, but at his hard look, I sink to the chair, perching on the edge. It's a tiny rebellion, but it's all the fight I have left.

"I don't fuck students. Ever. I told you that. And yes, Miss Bowen was definitely flirty, playing up the damsel in distress act, but I don't give a shit about that. I'm here to help and that's it." I open my mouth to say something, hating that I was right, but he talks over me, not giving me a breath to speak. "You have nothing to worry about. I have never touched a student, never fucked a student . . . until you. And I fought that tooth and nail until I couldn't fight anymore."

I settle a bit, the fire in my gut dying to embers at his reassuring words.

"I told you there were no second chances, that you are mine. The same is true for me, Daisy. I'm yours. And as sexy as your coming in here all full of jealousy over me may be, it's not safe. You look like an avenging angel, a possessive bitch, and fuck, do I love that. But it's not smart, not while we're way past the line of what's okay. You know we could both get in trouble for this." His words are hard, but his voice has gone quiet as he reprimands me. The softness is what hits home just how stupidly I was behaving. Anyone could've seen my obviously jealous fit, although Sabrina was the most likely person to bust me and she seemed oblivious. Thank God.

I duck my chin. "I'm sorry, Connor. I saw red when she was talking to you, so clearly flirting. And then she was dressed all sexy when she left your office in a better mood. I couldn't stand it. You're mine too." I let my eyes lift, meeting his with the declaration. I feel like there's more to say, the words tempting on my tongue, but I hold them tightly.

"Show me," he says. It's becoming a common demand and I love it. I lift an eyebrow questioningly. I'll show him whatever he wants to see, but I'm not sure what he wants right now.

"Show me how sorry you are. Show me that you're mine and I'm yours, Daisy." It's a challenge, an order, a sign of just how angry he is at my bratty behavior. This is a punishment and I know it. But it's one I'll gladly take.

I search my head for a moment, finding inspiration. I drop to the floor, crawling the few steps to beside his chair. He turns, watching me curiously as I approach. I kneel at his feet, sitting back on my heels between his spread knees, and reach for his jeans. Making quick work of them, I pull his boxers down, letting his cock spring free.

He's thick and hard for me. A thought wiggles in my mind, wondering if he was hard when Sabrina was here, but I force it away. He is mine, this cock is mine, and I don't want either of us to ever forget it again.

I lap at his head, tasting the salty velvet of his skin. I don't go slow this time, don't wait for him to take over and fuck my mouth. No, this time, I'm in charge, and I want to show him everything I feel without words . . . the possessiveness, the need, the love. I admit the word to myself, knowing that it's too fast, but that doesn't make it any less true.

I feast on him, taking him deep into my throat almost immediately and holding him there as I swallow. It feels odd, but when he grunts, his hands spearing into my hair, it's worth it so I do it again. "Fuck, Daisy."

I retreat to his tip, teasing along his slit to get the

precum, the appetizer to what I want so desperately. "You like that?""

He grins at me, arrogance in his order. "Do it again."

I almost obey. And then I think better of it. "What if I have something better in mind?"

His hand in my hair tightens as he holds my head still, bending down to rumble against my ear. "Better than my cock down your throat as you massage my tip with your muscles, swallowing like a needy girl even though I haven't given you my cum yet? Better than that?"

Fuck.

"Let's see what you think," I tease. I lift my hair, pulling my necklace off. It's just a costume length of pearls, but they're of good quality so they're smooth. I untie the knot I'd looped into the necklace this morning, delighted that Connor is watching me with interest. Slowly, I wrap the beads around his pulsing shaft, careful not to get them too tight. I need them to move against, not pinch, his sensitive skin. I take a moment to admire him with the new adornment, jacking him off slowly and peeking up to see his face awash in pleasure.

I let a dribble of spit out to lube along his shaft, coating the pearls and his skin. Then I take him, beads and all, into my mouth, spreading the saliva along him to ease my way. Once he's slippery, I focus my tongue's attention on his crown, letting my hands work the pearls up and down his length.

As I stroke him, I taunt him. "What do you think? Is my necklace wrapped around you as I jack you off into my hungry mouth better? Or maybe you want me to stop? Take the beads off and just lick you a bit?"

Connor's head lifts from where it'd fallen back in the chair. His eyes are wide. "Holy shit, Daisy. I've never . . . that feels amazing. Squeeze me tighter."

The victory rings between my legs, the thought that I'm making him this gone turning me on. I squeeze him tighter, rubbing the pearls up and down his shaft as I suck hard on his tip, hollowing my cheeks to make a vacuum. He fucks my hand, both of us working together to get him there.

And then he hisses, forcing my head down his shaft as he comes deep in my throat. I swallow over and over, wanting every drop. "Fuck, yes." When I've gotten every pulse of his cum, I lick my way up his shaft and carefully unwind the necklace.

Connor grabs a tissue from his desk, offering it to me. I wipe down the length of pearls and then slip it back over my head, retying the length so that the knot hits right in my cleavage.

Connor fingers the pearls, following the line up to the satin skin of my neck, where he wraps his fingers around my throat, not tight but letting me know he's there. "I think tonight, I'm going to give you a pearl necklace of a different sort. Would you like that, Daisy?"

I nod, my throat working against his palm when I swallow.

"Good girl. I'll see you tonight. Be at my place at seven again." Even at the praise and invitation, I deflate a bit.

I didn't think we were done here. I'm so fucking wet, my pussy needy for him. I squirm in my clothes, the cotton and denim too rough on my sensitive skin.

He smirks, and I realize this is part of the punishment too. He's making me wait on purpose. "Remember, nobody touches you but me, not even you."

I have a flash of wildness, but he sees it in my eyes. "And I'll know if you do, and I'll make you wait even longer."

Shit. I'm not gonna tempt him to punish me that much. A spank here, a delay there, I can take and even enjoy. But something tells me that if Connor really got going on denying my orgasm, I'd be begging long before he'd give in.

"Yes, sir," I say sarcastically. Okay, so I'm not going to give in sweetly, even if I am buckling with desire for what he's offering.

I get up from the floor, dusting imaginary bits from my knees. I grab my bag and make to leave, but right before I open the door, he speaks. "And, Daisy?"

I turn around to see he's got a huge shit-eating grin on his face. "Apology accepted." He winks at me.

I fight the urge to beam at the silly praise, knowing that the anger of the sex and the punishment was all in fun, even if the overreaction on my part was so very real. I curtsy slightly, holding out an imaginary skirt, "Thank you, sir. See you tonight. I can't wait."

We both grin, and I close the door behind me, a spring in my step as I head to my last class of the day.

CHAPTER 8

CONNOR

I'm trying my damnedest to wrap things up quickly, wanting to hit the gym with Nick before heading home to meet Daisy, when there's a knock on my door.

"Come in," I say, wishing whoever it is would go away so I can bail sooner rather than later. The thought is amplified when the door swings open and I see Dean Michaels in the doorway.

Fuck, does it smell like sex in here? Is he going to take one whiff of my office and know exactly what I've been doing? The obvious question if he realizes would be 'with whom?' and that's the most dangerous inquiry I could face.

"Dean Michaels, come in," I say, standing and offering a hand. He shakes mine and sits.

"Hey, Connor, how's the world of mathematics treating you?" It's his usual opening, but something feels off. Or maybe that's my conscience talking.

"It's pretty radical," I joke back, the same as always. What can I say, math jokes are rarely funny, but we all tell them just the same.

He smiles his usual politician smile. He's a man of few words. He told me once that he can't be misquoted if he rarely speaks. But he's smart and has run this department for decades, seeing and doing almost everything in his tenure. Something tells me he hasn't gotten a pearl necklace blowjob in his office though. Although if you'd asked me that a couple of weeks ago, I wouldn't have believed I'd ever say yes to that either.

"I heard the exciting news just now and wanted to be the first to congratulate you. Great job, Connor!" He offers a golf clap, obviously proud. "We're lucky to have you here, and I recognize that. Just remember that when the other universities start headhunting you, okay?"

He's blowing smoke up my ass, but I have no idea why. "I'll certainly remember that, sir. But I'm afraid I've missed something. What exactly are you congratulating me on?"

He chuckles. "They haven't contacted you yet? Well shit, guess I let the cat out of the bag then, didn't I? No more Schrodinger's Paradox here. The cat's alive, for damn sure." I still have no idea what he's talking about, though I'm familiar with Schrodinger's cat theory, both in the colloquial pop-culture reference and the more complex Copenhagen interpretation of quantum mechanics way.

He takes pity on me, finally explaining. "I got a call today from the TED talks people. It seems they're doing some final research on a proposed presenter and wanted my input, a reference, if you will. They're research-ing you, Connor."

My mind whirls. Holy Shit! "That's amazing, sir. No, I haven't heard a thing, but that'd be such an honor." It really is. TED talks are known as a way to bring complex subjects to the everyday person, a way to revo-lutionize our thinking about almost every topic on earth. An opportunity to speak on mathematics would be a great privilege, and partnered with my publishing, it would almost definitely make me a shoe-in for tenure, here or anywhere I wanted to go.

"Just remember where you come from when the time's right, Connor. I'll take good care of you here. You're doing great work with the students, and more impor-tantly, you bring attention to the mathematics program with your publishing, opportunities like this, and your willingness to play trained monkey at fundraisers." His voice is serious again, politician-style in full effect.

I grin. "Can't say I've ever been called a trained monkey as a compliment, but I get where you're coming from. Not many of the math team are willing to schmooze with the pocketbooks for financial support, and I'm decent enough at it, so I don't mind."

He nods. "Good. Let me know when they contact you and it's a done deal. I'll add it to your tenure proposal for this year before the committee meeting."

He stands, offering me a hand this time and then leav-ing. In the quiet of my office, I can see my future laid out before me. TED talks, tenure, publishing, research, teaching. All of it exactly what I'd always wanted, always dreamed about.

But now there's more to my dreams. As wild as it may sound, I want all that plus Daisy. I want her by my side for everything. Hell, once she's finished school, maybe we could even work together? The thought makes me grin. I'd reward her every solution with orgasms, thank her for hard work with my hands and tongue, and celebrate every milestone with my cock deep in her pussy. I think we'd work together quite beautifully.

I'm lost in the fantasy of what a shared life might look like when I hear a cleared throat from the doorway. "Ahem . . ."

I shake my head, clearing the rosy haze from my vision to see Nick leaning against the doorframe, grinning. "Lost in thought there, Mister Math?"

I smile back. "A bit. Got some good news and was imagining what it might be like if it's true."

His eyes spread wide. "Well, spill it. What's the good news?"

I consider telling him about the TED talk. Hell, I consider telling him about Daisy. He's my best friend, and though I'm well aware of how stupid what I'm doing is, there's a part of me that wants to shout it from the rooftops. I'm proud that she's mine, and hiding it feels like I'm ashamed. I'm not, but the consequences are dire. So I keep my mouth shut. "I can't tell yet. Don't want to jinx it. But as soon as I can, I'll let you know."

I know I'm talking about the TED talk more than Daisy. I don't know how long it'll be before we can let that particular cat of the bag. Sorry, Schrodinger.

"Alright, man. But I'm here whenever you're ready, and it sounds like the first round is on me to celebrate. You ready to hit the gym?" That's one of the reasons I love Nick, lame jokes aside. He's here to support me and cheer when something good happens, but he's a no-pressure type. If I need to disappear for weeks on end to work on something, he gets it because he's the same way. We've had each other's backs for a while now, and I appreciate that.

But right now, I don't want to work out. I want to get home, be that much closer to Daisy coming over so I can tell her the good news. She's who I really want to share this with, whether it actually comes through and happens or not.

"Sorry, man. Think I'm going to head home today. I'm too wired to work out. I'd be a shitty spotter, even if you're a lightweight," I tease.

Nick grins. "Fuck you. You know I lift more than you any day of the week." He's right, but I'm not going to tell him that. His ego's already bigger than mine, and that's saying something considering my ego's magnitude.

We both laugh, and he leaves, promising to make me lift twice as long next week to make up for the skipped session. That's fine by me if it gets me home to Daisy right now.

CHAPTER 9

DAISY

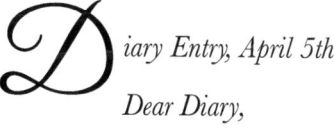 *iary Entry, April 5th*

Dear Diary,

It's been three weeks and I still can't quite believe it. Three weeks of secret rendezvous, praying we don't get caught, and pushing boundaries. It's been amazingly hot but also beautifully addicting.

My grades are even better, not because he's going easy on me but because under his tutelage, I really feel more confident in myself. He makes me feel empowered. It's me, my body, my personality, my heart, my intelligence . . . all that makes me Daisy Phillips that brought this man to his knees in a way he'd never even considered.

That confidence extends to the bedroom, although we rarely make it there, usually collapsing to the couch in his living room as soon as I walk in the door, at least for round one before slipping into his satin sheets. More than once, we've risked exposure by fucking in his office, but so far, we've been lucky and no one has caught on to us.

But it's not just my body. More than anything, my mind is filled with thoughts of him. I feel like a cliché, but the physical connec-

tion has ignited an emotional one I'd never dreamed of. I've learned so much about him, revealed so much about myself . . . and each tidbit only brings us closer. We spend hours making love, and then just as many talking. His brain turns me on almost as much as his amazing body. Actually, his mind probably is the sexiest part of him, but I won't tell him that or he might withhold his body from me as punishment. And I don't want that because I want him. Body, mind, and soul.

I'll be honest. It may be fast, but I think I've fallen in love with him.

I'M HIS. TOTALLY.

The thought is on repeat in my head as I head toward the math building, looking forward to my class with Connor. It seems strange to still be thinking about our first night now that we've been together for a few weeks, but that night was perfect and started a string of perfect days that hasn't stopped since.

It's just hard to believe that I lost my virginity to my professor. But he's more than that, and after the past weeks of our getting together every opportunity we can, of texting and chatting when we can't, I'm reassured that I am more than a conquest to him, that this is something else.

The experience has been beyond exciting, beyond exhilarating for both of us, it seems, from how he acts. I told him that since our first night, every pleasure sensor in my body has come alive, and I notice the little things more than ever. I'm aware of the swaying wideness of my hips and the way the air caresses my skin. Even the needy ache in my core reminds me of how he makes me come so hard, over and over again. Even now, I feel like every time is a new adventure, one I'll never get tired of.

The only bad part is my hunger for Connor, for the way his eyes look as we talk about the little things, for the way his eyes bore into me as he pounds his amazing cock inside me. I want him, *need* him with a fiery intensity, a deep, primal need to explore just who and what we can be together.

I'm so engaged in my fantasy, not even paying attention as I walk along the path to class, that it takes me a moment to realize someone's calling my name. "Daisy!"

I turn and see Arianna approaching me, a look of wonder on her face. "Oh, hi, Ari. Sorry, I was daydreaming. I missed you this morning."

"Must be fantasizing about a special someone," she says, smirking. "For the past few weeks, I don't think I've ever seen you look so happy."

"No, it's not that," I quickly lie. "I'm just feeling good about my classes. Things are ramping up well for finals. If I can keep it up, my early slip shouldn't matter."

"Really?" she says, sighing. "That's all it is? Because I've noticed your late-night 'study sessions' and weekend sleepovers with 'a friend'. I'm not stupid, Daisy." I can tell that I've hurt her with my secrecy and silence. She knows something's going on, and usually, I tell her everything, but not this. I can't.

"I'm sorry, Ari. I am seeing someone, but I'm not ready

to talk about it. I can't. Please understand, chica." I beg her to not press this, knowing it could cause problems. My first loyalty is to Connor now, and I won't put him at jeopardy over a need to share with my best friend.

She smiles sweetly. "Okay, I'll leave it be on one condition." I nod, and she continues, "Does he make you happy?"

I don't even try to restrain my huge smile. "So happy, Ari." My voice is high and light, the buzz of happiness filling me and apparent.

"All right, then, I'm here when you're ready to dish all the good stuff. As long as he's not some old geezer professor, married, and with bad breath, who likes to listen to the sound of his own voice." She's teasing, but I flinch a bit when she says *professor*. None of the rest of her description fits Connor at all, but that one is dangerously close to the truth, and I need to redirect her to safer territory.

"Definitely not. What about you? I have been gone a lot lately, so I feel like I don't know what's going on with you either. Classes? Internship? Spill it, girl!"

She takes the bait, and we dissolve into a catch-up session of epic proportions as we walk the sidewalks to our classes, enjoying the sunshine and the company. I have missed her these last few weeks as my focus has been locked onto Connor. It's not a bad thing, just the excitement of something new, and he definitely takes up all the space in my head and my heart.

"So I should be good on all my classes, just finals to worry about mostly. And I finally heard back from

Morgan, and I start there soon," Ari tells me, excitement obvious as she dances around. *See?* I think. *She's excited about something new too.* We're all good. Just part of growing up and apart a bit as our paths wind and diverge and reconnect.

"I'm so glad, girl. You're gonna ace your tests and impress the hell out of them at Morgan. I'm good on tests too. I've got an *A*-minus in Professor Daniels's class now, so unless I bomb the final, I should have a solid *B*-plus or better final grade. I'm more worried about American History at this point. I have an *A*, but the test is all essay, no multiple-choice, and a bad grade there can tank the whole semester."

We get to the division point in our paths, Ari needing to go left to the business building and me needing to head right to math.

She grabs me in a spontaneous hug. "Dang, I needed that. I'm here for you, honey. Whenever you're ready to spill, I'm ready to listen and support and celebrate. I'll see you at home later?"

I laugh. "It's good to see you too, and I know you've got my back. I've got yours too. Anytime and always, girl. I uh . . . don't know about tonight, though." I stutter a bit on the words, not wanting to lie but not wanting to give away too much.

Her grin is like the cat that got the canary, "That's okay. Go get you some. Bow-chicka-bow-wow," she sing-songs as she walks away.

She's right. I needed that too. I have been so tied up with Connor that I've let other things fall through the cracks. Before I can promise myself that I'll do better, the thought of being *tied up with Connor* fills my mind with some rather dirty images of just what I want to do with my professor, and maybe what I want him to do with me too.

CHAPTER 10

CONNOR

*C*ollapsing into a chair in the break room, my body's exhausted even as my head feels like it's about ready to explode. I shouldn't have any caffeine, but I slurp at today's drink, a double espresso instead of my normal macchiato.

She's my every fantasy come to life. A brain that commands my respect, sweet but mischievous . . . and her magical pussy is literally the cherry on top of a perfect sundae. I've never, in my wildest fantasies about Daisy, thought we'd end up fucking in my office . . . but now it seems as natural as breathing.

I do know that she puts a smile on my face, something I'm not particularly known for, I guess, considering the dean's secretary asked what had me in such a good mood as we discussed next year's PhD candidate program in the elevator.

I'm troubled now, though, which is why I'm sucking down caffeine like it's water. Simply put, it's not enough.

I want more. *Need* more.

I need to know that the look I see in her eyes as she kisses me goodbye and the little teasing in her voice as we hurriedly talk about when we can get together next aren't just figments of my imagination. My deepest fear about giving in to my desire for Daisy was that it'd be a one-time thing, a booby trap in my background that someone could use to blast me with when shit got tough.

But now, I'm even more scared . . . because I want something with her I've never wanted before. I want her mind, soul, and heart, not just her body.

"Hey amigo, you're looking grim," Nick says, breaking me out of my head. "The dean's fundraising shit got you that screwed up?"

"No, nothing like that," I assure him. "Just a little indigestion, I guess. Busy."

"Uh-huh. Well, here's some news that'll get your mind off that," Nick says, sitting down. "Cunningham resigned."

"No shit?" I comment, surprised. "He didn't hang onto his tenure?"

"Nope. Oh, they're calling it an extended sabbatical, but he's out, man. I figure he's digging himself a hole for when his wife's lawyers get done crucifying him," Nick says. "Oh, and his lover? Kicked his ass to the curb from the scuttlebutt. I know I've never been too fond of him, but still . . . shitty way to go out. Never want to see that happen."

I nod. I should probably be worried, but I'm not. Daisy would never say a word. Our . . . situation that seems to be developing at light speed is safe. Risky, but safe. Every moment I'm with her, I feel like instead of black jeans and a T-shirt, I'm wearing a Kevlar suit, a giant bat emblazoned on my chest. I'm fucking untouchable, man.

"It is a bad situation," I finally reply. "He's brilliant enough to still get grants and work privately, but this will be a side note in everything he does."

Dean Michaels comes in, giving Nick and me a wave. "Professor Daniels, when your office was empty, I figured I'd find you down here with your partner in crime," he says, shaking hands with the two of us. "I just wanted to say, the PhD board has come back with its initial comments on the theses they've gotten this year. Your students, as a whole, blew their socks off. Very, very impressive."

"Thank you, sir . . . but they're the ones who put in the work," I defer, but he's having none of it.

"Oh, of course, but their mentor deserves some kudos too. I hope your undergrads will be just as impressive."

"We'll have to see after finals, but I'm confident in them."

"In any case, congratulations," Michaels says. He watches as Nick gets up to refill his mug and then carefully asks, "Have you heard anything from TED?"

I shake my head. "Not yet. Although I had a previous

mentor contact me saying they'd called him too. Still research phase, it seems."

Michaels nods. "Very well. Good day, gentlemen."

He leaves, and I chug back as much of my espresso as possible in one gulp. It sits heavily in my belly, but I need the jumpstart to be at my best today.

CLASS IS WELL . . . CLASS. THEY SIT, I TALK, THEY listen, I teach. It's a good group of students, and like I told Dean Michaels, I'm confident in their work. But my mind is a million miles away. Or at least a hallway away, down in my office, with Daisy laid out on my desk as I pound into her.

But no, that's only in my mind. In reality, she's sitting front and center like always, eyes glued to me. It takes all my caffeinated control to hold back from kissing her.

As I wrap up, I give her a hard look that she seems to understand. I walk out of class, ignoring her as she leans against the wall, face buried in her phone. I wonder for a moment who she's talking to, but I realize it's probably for show.

I try to stay casual, exchanging greetings with other professors and students as I make my way to my office.

Barely a minute later, she knocks gently on my door that I left cracked for her, and as she comes in, I shut the door behind her, pressing her to the wood and capturing her cry of surprise with a hungry kiss. She seems just as hungry, the two of us devouring each other before the pure need for oxygen forces us apart slightly. "Twenty-four hours," she moans, thinking about the time since we last got together. "It's too long to be without you."

"I can't fucking get enough of you," I say, pressing my forehead to hers. "You're like a habit, but a fucking good one. I'm addicted to you after just this short of a time." There's more, but I don't want to say it here. She deserves more than that.

"Me too," she says, letting her hands slide down to my ass. "I thought talking on the phone last night would be enough to get me through class, but the moment I saw you, all I could think was how much I need you inside me."

"I want to ruin you," I admit, pulling her toward my desk. "I know it's too fast, but I don't want any other man to ever have you. You're mine, Daisy." I've told her that before, but it seems heavier in this moment, a taste of the bigger truth.

Her eyes shine, and I think she hears the words I'm not saying. "Take me. Ruin me. You're all I'll ever want."

She wiggles away from me, slipping her panties off and holding them out to me. An offering. Then she flips her skirt up, lying forward, her chest pressed to the wood. An even better offering on the altar of my desk. My sacrifice. My life. My everything.

She's already sloppy wet, the tease of being together but not able to touch for the last hour driving us both wild. I moan, unbuckling and pulling my cock out as I stand behind her. I grab her cheeks, savagely squeezing them in my hands as I spread her for a better view of her pink slit.

I lick at her, fucking her with my tongue and torturing her clit with fast flicks, needing her taste on my tongue as I fuck her. I rise, slipping through her folds, coating myself in her honey, and then I ease inside her, one inch at a time but not stopping until I'm balls-deep. I hold there, my cockhead pressed to her back wall, bottomed out, as she adjusts to the feeling of being so full.

"Yes," she hisses. She looks back at me over her shoulder. "You have all I am," she whispers, both of us dancing around the words we want to say.

I lean forward to kiss her, letting her know that I understand. And then I press her down, my hands pinning her to the desk. She whimpers, arching her back to let me know she's ready. I pull back and thrust in deeply, going as hard as I can without making too much noise.

"Touch yourself, Daisy," I command her. She shifts slightly, getting her right hand down to play with her clit. "That's it, honey. Take my cock in your tight little pussy and rub that clit for me."

She does as I say, both of us working her body, me from the inside and her from the outside. I watch as my cock disappears into her and reappears coated in her creamy honey. It's beautiful, and her surrender to me is glorious as she lets me ride her harder, pressing her so firmly into the desk that she can't move, can't fight the heat I'm building within her. She takes it, letting me split her with violent thrusts.

I lean forward, growling in her ear, "Give it to me, Daisy. Come on my cock like my good girl."

She cries out, the sound strangled as I rush to slam my hand over her mouth, stifling her sexy noises. If anyone hears, there'd be no doubt about what's happening in my office.

It's wrong, but the thought of someone catching us, of some poor schmuck student walking in and seeing me fucking ravaging innocent virginal Daisy Phillips, the class good girl, gives me a thrill. I'm the lucky fucker she chose to pop that cherry, and I'm the bastard who will keep this pussy full of my cock, and only my cock, for as long as she'll let me. I come hard, filling her deeply with my cum, marking her as mine.

I lay a kiss to her shoulder as I slip out, grabbing tissues as my cream leaks from her. She stands, spinning, and we seal our vows, both spoken and unspoken, with a kiss.

She tries to straighten the mess we've made of my desk, stacking papers and putting the stapler upright once again.

"What's this?" she asks, holding up a red envelope.

My eyebrows pull together. "I don't know. Let me see." She hands it to me and I open it. I pull out a folded sheet of paper as something flutters to the floor.

Daisy drops to the floor to pick it up and gasps. "Oh, my God!"

I take it from her hand and realize it's a picture. A picture of Daisy and me, here in my office. She's on her knees before me, head buried in my crotch, obviously mid-blowjob, and my head is thrown back in pleasure, my hands buried in her hair. It looks sexy as fuck. It looks like I'm forcing her. It looks like I'm fucking my student.

It looks like I'm . . . fucked.

CHAPTER 11

DAISY

"*We* have to go, need to get out of here and figure out what the fuck is going on. Skip your next class and meet me at home," Connor tells me. He's all-business, hard and brooking no argument.

I'm frozen, eyes locked on the picture. He grabs my head, cradling it his hands roughly. "Daisy, honey . . . look at me. Go to my house. It's going to be okay, but we need to talk this through, and we're obviously compromised here. You okay?" I must nod because he lets me go and picks up my bag and places it on my shoulder, but he pauses with a hand on the doorknob and turns back. "It'll be okay, I promise," he tells me before placing a sweet kiss to my forehead.

Outside, I hurry along the sidewalk. I've always felt safe here. Hell, I probably felt a bit *too* comfortable, considering the mess I've gotten into now. But as I scurry to the corner, waiting for the bus to take me across town to Connor's, I feel like there are eyes on me from every direction, like there's a big sign over my head that's blinking, *Fucking Her Professor*, and everyone can see it but me. The little bubble of happiness I've been living in for weeks just burst spectacularly, and now I feel exposed, vulnerable.

The bus ride is painfully slow, giving my brain all sorts of time to freak out, worry, and compose a million different scenarios. They all end badly . . . for me and for Connor.

By the time I walk up to his door, I'm verifiably a ball of nerves, looking over my shoulder and wondering if it'd be better if I just went to the dorm and we pretended none of this ever happened. But I can't do that. I don't care if I'm screwed over. I can always change schools if I have to. But I won't leave Connor to face the firing squad at school alone. I'll do whatever I have to do to protect his career because that's not as easy as switching universities. He'll be blackballed and his reputation as a student-fucker will precede him. Even if it's not like that, not really. I mean, I *am* his student, but this is more than some naughty taboo. This is real.

I don't even get the chance to knock before he rips the door open and pulls me inside. At first, I think it's so no one will see me, but he immediately presses me to the door and takes my mouth in a kiss. Between smacks, he asks, "How're you doing, honey? Are you freaking out?"

I nod, feeling the tears wet my lashes. "I'm so sorry, Connor. I know we shouldn't have in your office, but I thought we were okay. Your career, this is going to ruin you, isn't it?" I'm rambling, verging on hysterical. But he's steady, calm, a port in the storm ravaging us.

"Come on, Daisy. Sit down so we can talk." His words don't inspire confidence, and I'm almost certain this is the point where he tells me this has been fun, but he needs to think of himself now. But dutifully, I sit on the couch, bending my legs and hugging my knees to my chest.

He sits down beside me and tosses back the shot of Scotch sitting on the table before burying his head in his hands. "Fuck. I knew something like this could happen. But I got careless, so wrapped up in being with you. I knew better. I fucking knew better. Now, I'm going to be just like Cunningham. Even now, we're taking a risk with you in my house, but I couldn't think of a safer place." He's talking to me, but his words seem more to himself, castrating himself over what we've done.

It takes every bit of my strength, but I'll do anything for him. I scoot closer to him, my nails tracing soothing patterns on his back. "I'm so sorry, Connor. Tell me what to do and I'll do it. I can tell the dean that I seduced you, that it's my fault. Whatever you need so that your job is secure. I'll switch schools. Anything you need."

He lifts his head, looking at me strangely. "What are you talking about?" he asks angrily.

I duck my head, not able to meet his eyes when I say the words. "I figure this meant you'd switch into self-preservation mode, and rightfully so. I'm willing to do whatever you need me to so that you're safe at work. I can switch schools a hell of a lot easier than you, and then maybe you won't get fired."

Understanding dawns, and he smiles slightly, even at this scary moment. "Daisy, I'm not throwing you under the bus to save myself. *We* did this, and I want to keep doing it. We'll figure it out together."

Hope blooms in my chest. "Really?"

He pulls me into his lap, grabbing my head and forcing my eyes to his. "Daisy, it's you and me. I told you that you're mine. Nothing changes that. I love you."

He doesn't give me time to process what he said. He just covers my mouth with a kiss, promising that things are going to be okay and that we have a future beyond some taboo naughty affair. But as his tongue tangles with mine, the words settle in my heart, lighting me up and giving me strength. I pull back. "I love you too, Connor. So much."

And then we seal my words to him with another kiss. It's beautiful. It's amazing. It's something I thought I'd never find, much less find with my professor.

And someone wants to take this away from us.

Connor rests his forehead against mine, our breath mingling. "I know this may be a stupid question . . . but have you told anyone about us?"

I look at him, glancing at the photo on the table before shaking my head slowly. "Not even Arianna knows. She sorta knows I had a crush on you, but that's it. She would always be the one pushing my buttons about it, teasing me a little."

"Would there be any reason for her to follow you and

want to do this? She wouldn't want to hurt you, would she?"

I shake my head as I think for a moment. "No," I finally say. "If anything, Ari would be the one person I could actually trust with our relationship. I can't imagine her being anything but supportive. She's . . . she's pretty fucking awesome, really. But I didn't think it was fair to you, so I kept it a secret."

"Okay. Well, we're going to have to lie low," Connor replies, obviously wishing the solution were so easy. "It's like any math problem. Until the variables are identified, the problem is unsolvable."

And just like that, a switch in my gut flips and I'm not scared. I'm furious. "How dare they? Why are we being forced to lie low when we're not doing anything wrong? Not really. We're two consenting adults." I know my voice is reaching a fevered pitch, but the anger is burning hot.

"If only it were that easy. But I think you know that. I'm talking about more than the law. If people find out about our relationship at the university, there are serious consequences for both of us. Though maybe a little more for me. I may be asked to resign, and if not that, I'm certainly going to be pigeonholed. My reputation would be ruined. More than that, so would yours. I can live with being seen as some horny professor who couldn't resist the temptation. I can make a living in the private sector. But you . . . you're just getting started."

My face crumples as his words sink in, and for a moment, I think the tears are going to overflow.

"I know, honey. I understand, but don't cry. Your tears are like a knife in my gut."

I wipe the tears from my cheeks, not wanting to hurt him any further. "Connor . . . I don't know how to deal with all this. I feel like I just found happiness. I found the man I want to be with . . . and now this."

"I wish I could lie and say that somehow it'll all work out, but I'm not a good liar." He takes my hand, kissing my fingertips. "But what I can say is that I want to be with you, too. But if there's even a chance of that, we need to figure out what this person wants. I mean, there's no note, no blackmail demand, which is what I'd expect. So who's sneaking around to take this picture of us? I need you to think really hard about who this could be. Because I've racked my brain, and I'm drawing nothing."

He holds me tightly, my head resting on his shoulder and his finger teasing along the skin of my thighs. I sigh. "I don't know who it could be. Why anyone would try to take this away from us . . . but Connor . . ."

I lift up, meeting his green eyes. "Firestorm aside, we just had a really important moment." I dip my chin, biting my lip and feeling stupid for needing this right now as an unknown person tries to rip everything apart, but it's the truth. "I love you. I need you." The words couldn't be simpler. The truth couldn't be more complex.

He swallows, squeezing the flesh of my thighs with his strong fingers. "I love you, and I need you too," he says, repeating my truths. "I didn't think it'd happen, and not this fast, but I want to do nothing more than explore you, to discover the little things that make you laugh, and what type of eggs you like in the morning, or if you hate eggs and prefer pancakes or cereal or . . . whatever. I'm rambling, but I want that forever."

His eyes shine bright with the honesty of his statement, and I realize that we've both been holding back. This is more, just like he promised at the beginning. So much more. This is now and tomorrow and the day after that. He is my forever, regardless of what that forever might look like after we deal with the asshole trying to take it away from us.

Facing the firing squad together. That's what we'll have to do. But right now, I need to tell my man that I love him with my body, not just my words. And I want him to do the same, show me with his talented fingers and thick cock just how much he feels for me.

Connor sweeps me up in his arms, carrying me down the hall to his bedroom and tossing me lightly to the bed before following me, covering my body with his. Quickly stripping, we lie together, eyes locked on one another, more bare emotionally than physically. Without preamble, he enters me and we become one. We make love this time, soft and slow and sweet, tangled in the satin of his bed, our words repeated time and time again as we come together. I hear his love, feel his love, and I know he feels mine for him as well.

CHAPTER 12

*W*alking into work the next day is weird. I'm looking over my shoulders the whole time, evaluating whether there's something sinister behind every friendly smile and greeting, looking for anyone who might be watching me. I completely skip the breakroom, though I could definitely use something stronger than my office pot's weak-ass coffee. But going in there seems like a needless risk right now.

How crazy is that? Getting coffee in the breakroom is . . . risky? Whose life is this?

But the truth is, I don't know who's doing this, and until I rule out that it's another professor, I don't want to give them potential ammunition or be alone in a room with them. Honestly, I'm not sure what I'd do if I found out, but the fury raging through my veins says I should probably play it safe and sip on the sludge I call coffee.

I stand tall as I go into my office, refusing to shrink under this pressure or sneak around. Yeah, maybe Daisy and I have been sneaking, although rather poorly, apparently, but that was out of necessity. I'm not ashamed of her, of myself, or of what we have. But still, the instinct to hide to avoid the shitstorm remains.

What's the saying? 'Courage is not the absence of fear, but rather the assessment that something else is more important than the fear.' That's Franklin Roosevelt, I believe, though I'm more math nerd than historical literary scholar. But the sentiment is true, because I'm scared as fuck that this is all going to implode, leaving bits of my career and Daisy's future scattered about. But I won't hide what we are, what we want to be, because there is nothing more important than Daisy.

But as I close the door behind me, needing a moment alone, all my strength is tested when I see that there's another red envelope on the floor. Fuck. Someone must've slipped it under the door. I pick it up gingerly, like it's a bomb that might blow up my life, and sit down at my desk.

Opening it, I see that there's no picture this time, just a single sheet of standard copy paper with plain typed text.

48 hours. $100,000 to my bank account. Straight As in your classes until I graduate. Or I go public and expose what you've been doing, Naughty Professor. Meet me at the Golden Wok on Poplar Street on Thursday at 7 P.M. to discuss. —S

What the fuck? What the actual fuck?

The money strikes me first. I don't have that kind of money. I mean, I could liquidate some stocks and shit, but that's a fuckton of money to a professor, not something I have lying around or can get in forty-eight fucking hours.

It takes a heartbeat for the rest to register. Straight *A*s? That means . . . it's a student, not a coworker. Some little shit student is doing this to Daisy and me. And for what? Like an *A* in my class is worth destroying someone's life over? How utterly ridiculous. Like Mommy and Daddy won't be happy if Junior gets anything less than a perfect score that he obviously didn't earn?

Disgust fills me, followed hotly by the desire to figure out who this fucker is and destroy him. I mentally run through my class rosters, trying to remember names that start with S. Let's see, there's . . . Sam in my 9 A.M. trigonometry class, Scott in my graduate program, Sean is my 3 P.M. calculus class, and the list goes on and on. Steven, Seth, Simon, Sergio, Sebastian. Fuck. How many students' names even start with *S*? It's nothing I've paid attention to before, but now the suspect list is growing exponentially.

I stuff the envelope into my bag, needing to get to class. The last thing I need when the shit hits the fan is to be seen as unreliable on top of everything else.

When I go into the classroom, I can't help but look at Daisy in the front row. She'd put on a brave face this morning as she left my place and looks beautiful as always, but I can see the fray around the edges. Her hair is pulled up, tendrils escaping down like she couldn't be bothered to care. I want to wrap them around my finger and whisper in her ear that it's going to be okay just like I did last night as she fell asleep in my arms. She's wearing leggings and a long T-shirt. Actually, at a second glance, she's wearing *my* Batman T-shirt. Damn, I'm not so sure that was a good idea, but I love the way she looks in my clothes, like she's mine. Still, the Batman logo reminds me of my earlier feeling of being untouchable and just how naïve I was in thinking that.

I get started, going over prep review for the upcoming final. I do my best, but I stumble a couple of times and I know the students are getting pissed that I'm fucking up their last shot at help before the big test. I'm usually clear and precisely on point, so the difference is noticeable, but my brain is too busy with bigger things to concentrate on. I give in, closing the time with a promise. "If you study your notes from the semester, go over your previous tests, and complete the practice problems, you will be ready. I'll be in the online portal as much as possible over the next few days to help with any questions you may have." That seems to pacify them a bit.

As everyone files out, I hear them coordinating study group dates, and I'm thankful for the good group of students I have. Well, all except for one asshole.

Daisy stays back, waiting until everyone is gone. I glance at the door, making sure we're alone but knowing that's simply an illusion now, and we need to be careful because who knows what prying eyes are watching? I grab the envelope from my bag and sit down in the chair next to her. She leaves the book open on her desk, giving the impression that I'm merely helping with classwork.

I hand her the envelope and her eyes widen. "Oh, shit. Another one?"

She opens it and reads it silently before her eyes flash

back to mine. "Fuck, Connor! That's a crazy amount of money!" she exclaims, though she's working to keep her voice quiet. "What are we going to do? Do you even have that kind of money? I mean, I never even thought about what a professor makes, but that sounds like . . . a lot."

I nod. "It is a lot. I could get my hands on it, but it'd take everything I have, and the reality is that blackmail never ends. If I give in this time, they'll just keep asking for more."

"This is like some movie, not real life. Not my life. My mind is overloaded, like everything is white noise, and I can't isolate a clear path or process to find a solution."

That's my girl. Everything relates back to math for her. Hell, and for me. Maybe that's the key. Treat this like a math problem and solve the fucking thing. I'd had this thought before, reducing the variables. But there are so many.

The first of which is who the blackmailer is. Actually, maybe Daisy can help with that.

"Hey, so let's work with what we know. It's a student. We didn't know that before, but asking for grades makes that obvious. I've been running through my mind for which of my students start with *S*, but there are tons of them . . . Seth, Scott, Sean. Too many guys to narrow it down, really."

Her eyes go wide with shock. "Oh, my God!" I've seen that expression on her face before, when she has a revelation about how to solve a problem in class in a new way. Although this time, there's a hint of pain and disgust. "It's Sabrina."

My eyebrows snap together, putting the puzzle pieces together even as she keeps talking. "It's her, Connor. She's struggling in class, and she needs the grade for her scholarship. Hell, she needs the money. And she wasn't here today. It's gotta be her."

"Shit. I think you're right. It's her." I agree with her assessment, even though I hate the thought. "She's always seemed nice enough, a hard worker, and I know she was going to study group."

Daisy cringes. "Yeah, I told her to ask for help and even suggested that maybe she join another study group. Hell, I even helped her with a process she was doing incorrectly. I guess she found another way." Her tone is snide, obviously hating that Sabrina is taking the easy way out at our expense.

"Okay, so that's one big variable solved. What else?"

It's like a light is flipped on, and I know the answer. Daisy. She's the most important thing to me.

I can't cave in. Doing so would be selling her out, cheapening what we have, and that's unacceptable. I know what I need to do.

"Connor?" Daisy asks, her hands practically shaking as she reaches out to touch mine before she pulls back and glances at the door. "You went quiet. What are we going to do?"

The fear in her voice pisses me off. Not at her, but at Sabrina, who thought taking something as beautiful as our love and running it through the wringer as some tawdry, shameful thing was a valid way to salvage a bad grade.

"I'm here, Daisy. I'm just simplifying," I tell her, trying to come up with a better term, but it's the most accurate for what I'm planning. "I know what to do."

She sputters. "What?"

I can't tell her exactly what I'm thinking. She'll try to talk me out of it. I know she will because that's who she is, a sweet and kind-hearted woman who will sacrifice herself to save me. But I'll do anything for her.

I kiss her forehead, not caring if anyone sees. "It's okay, honey. I've got this. Go home to your dorm tonight, and I'll pick you up tomorrow night to go to Sabrina's requested *appointment*." The word is ugly on my tongue.

She looks at me, caution in her eyes. "What are you going to do?"

"I love you, Daisy. You're mine and I'm yours. And no one is going to take that away from us." I lay one light kiss to her hand before letting go and walking out of the classroom. It's one of the hardest things I've ever done because my every instinct is to huddle her to my side and never let her leave the security of my arms. But I need to fix this . . . for me, for her, for us.

I KNOCK ON THE DOOR, STEELING MYSELF WITH A DEEP breath. The rumbled 'Come in' from the other side sounds like a death knoll, but I approach with courage, choosing Daisy over the fear, over all else.

"Connor! I wasn't expecting to see you. Did I miss an appointment?" Dean Michaels asks, glancing to the paper calendar on his desk. Old school to the end, that's him.

"No, sir. But something's come up and I need to talk to you," I say, sitting down in front of him without an invitation.

"Of course. I've got a few minutes for you. This is about the TED talk, I'm guessing," he says, taking a sip of his coffee, and I frown. What I'm about to say could fuck that up too, but so be it.

"No, still haven't heard back on that yet. But there's something serious I need to discuss." I take a breath, wishing there were an easy way to say this, but there's simply not. "Dean, I've been seeing a student. It's . . . intimate."

His face freezes for a moment, then he sets his mug of coffee down and considers me carefully. "Connor, if this is some attempt at a joke, I really wish you'd picked a better time. Pre-exam pranks are the sort of thing students do, not professors."

"It's not a joke," I reply. "Her name's Daisy Phillips, and she's an undergrad. We've been seeing each other for a good part of the semester."

The dean taps his finger on his desk for a few moments, looking like he's going to explode. Finally, in a strained, tense voice, he speaks. "And did it ever occur to you that sleeping with a student could cost you your job? Haven't you heard the news? Cunningham?"

"I know, sir. It just happened. It's . . . we're serious."

Michaels nods, rubbing at his face. "Have you given her an unfair advantage at all in your class? Not that you can even answer that impartially." He sighs.

"No!" I exclaim before forcing myself under control. "No. If anything, I graded her harder than any of the other students. She's got an *A* in the class right now, but it's because she's one of the brightest minds I've ever come across."

Dean Michaels snorts. "Ever come across . . . you sound like an old geezer. I'm going to need full disclosure and every grade you've given her, all the records. According to school policy, there's nothing that can *legally* happen to you, but professionally, that's another story. I wouldn't be counting on that tenure, Connor."

"I understand, sir. Of course. I know that this is tantamount to career suicide for me, and I'll do whatever you need to maintain some semblance of a reputation. My main concern is Daisy." I look at him, all shreds of arrogance washed away in my desperation. "Can she transfer to another professor's roster, let them reevaluate her previous work, which they'll see is top-notch, and then she can take her final for them? I'll step out of the whole scenario so that she is able to complete her semester."

It's a big ask and I know it. Dean Michaels is well within his rights to wipe the entire credit from Daisy's transcript. Hell, he's probably able to kick her out of school.

If not outright, I'm sure he could call in a favor here or there to punish Daisy and me both.

He doesn't say yes, but he doesn't say no. And as the conversation continues, I have a sliver of hope that maybe this can all work out.

CHAPTER 13

DAISY

ear Diary, May 6th

How is it that heaven can turn into hell so quickly?

When I first started crushing on Connor, it was innocent. I mean, I never seriously thought that he and I would end up in bed together, and I certainly didn't think that we'd find such depth of feeling for each other.

And I never wanted our relationship to get him into trouble. I just wanted . . . him. Cocky, arrogant bastard and all.

And now my selfish desire has put his entire career at risk. We stepped over that forbidden line and there's no going back.

But I have to admit . . . as deep as we're in it right now, I've loved every minute of it. Of being his, of him being mine.

I don't know exactly what Connor has planned, but he told me he'd take care of us, and I believe him.

I CHECK THAT I HAVE ALL MY STUFF, ZIPPING MY BAG closed and sliding it over my shoulder. Gone are the flirty skirts or the tight jeans. I'm too frightened by yesterday's note. Besides, I slept like hell, my body just unable to handle the hours of ups and downs. We went from intense, passionate fucking to outright terror.

Connor and I swapped texts a few times, but there's a strain in what we say now, the two of us being unwilling to say anything over text about Sabrina's note. And though he told me he has a plan, which is supposed to put me at ease, I think, the fact that he won't tell me what it is makes me jumpy and nervous.

"Hey, chica, you okay?" Arianna asks as I clunk a bowl down on the counter to try and gobble some cereal. On top of everything else, I haven't eaten much in the past twenty-four hours, and now my head's sort of woozy, so college-norm breakfast for dinner is all I can muster. "You were riding the happy horse just a few days ago. Now you look like you've been told your puppy died."

No, it's like I've been sent an engraved invitation to a dance party in hell. And worst of all, despite this shit sundae that I've been served, my body's still craving Connor.

Instead of telling Ari this, of course, I just shake my head. "Been hitting the books a little too hard. Exams have me worried." Going to the fridge, I splash some milk on my Rice Krispies and turn to her. "What about you? Ready for finals?"

Before the words are even out of my mouth, I can see that she doesn't believe me. Hell, I don't believe me either.

"Nice attempt at deflection. Try again, Daisy. What's going on?" Ari demands, holding out a spoon for me. But as I go to grab it, she pulls it back. "Speak or no spoon."

I collapse to the chair, my bowl bouncing on the table and leaving a puddle of milk that I can't care to clean up. The tears well up unbidden. "Shit, honey. Here, take the spoon," Ari says, shoving it into my hand.

"It's not that. It's Professor Daniels," I mutter. Even calling him that now belies the depth of my feelings for him.

Ari looks at me questioningly. "I thought you said you were doing better in his class. Are you freaking about the final?"

It's on the tip of my tongue to lie, just tell her that the test is stressing me out. But I know Ari, and I was right when I told Connor that of anyone, she'd be the person I could trust most with this. But is it too dangerous to spill, especially not knowing what he has planned? Maybe being quiet about the whole thing is for the best, at least for now.

But I need support, and Ari is my best friend. I trust her. "No, not the final. I'm ready for that. It's . . . it's . . ."

She smiles encouragingly. "Spit it out. I'm here for you, no matter what. Maybe I can help."

"I've been seeing him. Professor Daniels—Connor —romantically."

Her eyes widen, "Holy shit, Daisy! You're fucking your math professor? Do you know how much trouble you could get into, how much trouble *he* could get into? Oh, my God, did he pressure you into this? That cocky fucker, I'll kill him." She's ranting, already in my defense like the true friend I knew she would be.

I place my hand on hers. "No, it's not like that. We're in love. I love him, Ari. And he loves me."

Her eyes search mine. "For real? You're in love with him? And he's in love with you?" Her voice is disbelieving, like I'm some silly school girl caught up in a fantasy.

"Ari, we're in love." She must see the truth now, because she gasps.

"Holy shit, Daisy," she repeats, seemingly her main response to this news. "That's . . . good? I mean, I guess. If you're both into it. But how? What now? I don't know what to say." We both stare at each other for a moment, my confession weighing the air down between us.

"Wait . . . if you're in love, then why the tears? What's wrong?" Ari asks, always astute.

"There's a girl in my class—"

"Mother fucker, I'll kill him," Ari interrupts.

"No, no, he's not . . . it's not like that. We're serious. He wouldn't do that. But this girl, she found out about us. And now . . ."

I give Ari the whole sordid story, from our initial flirtations to last night's text, explaining about Sabrina and the blackmail. Ari's face shows her every emotion, from excitement and sweet awwws to fury and homicidal mania.

"That bitch! How dare she? So, what are you going to do?" she asks.

"I don't know. Connor said he'd take care of it, but he hasn't filled me in on the plan beyond that he's picking me up for *dinner* at the Golden Wok." My frustration at the whole situation hides the deeper, darker fear at my core. "Ari, what if it's not okay? What if this gets out and ruins his career? I'll never forgive myself."

She smiles. "Chica, that right there tells me all I need to know. You're not worried for yourself. All you've talked about is him, how this will hurt him, and how you'll do anything he wants to make this right. If he feels even a bit of the same way, you two are going to be fine. It might not be the same fantasy future you'd imagined, but you'll be okay. I promise."

Her simple words, the innocent belief that it's going to work out, reassure me more than I would've imagined, giving me peace in a way I didn't realize I needed. I nod. "Thanks, Ari. I love you, girl."

She grins, wiping at the tracks of tears down my face. "No problem. That's what friends are for. Just remember this for my next crisis when I come crying to you, okay?"

I smile, the tight stretch of my face reminding me that smiles have been in short supply the last few days with all this drama. It feels good, more like myself. "Deal. Maybe come to me *before* the shit hits the fan though?"

Ari winks and my phone dings. "That's Connor, telling me that he's here. He's meeting me down the block because he's being extra-cautious." I sigh, wishing I could just walk down the steps and get into my boyfriend's car like any other regular woman.

"Go get him, girl. And go smack that bitch for me or I'll have to do it for you. Ugh . . . some people," Ari rants, rolling her eyes.

THE GOLDEN WOK IS ONE OF THOSE PLACES THAT becomes an institution around just about every college campus in America. It was first a local hangout for the counterculture and hippie movements before somehow becoming that place where students would meet up. Cheap food, friendly service, and a convenient location right outside the main gates of campus certainly helped, and when the original owner passed on, his son took over.

The Wok is a student place, and it's packed as we walk in. Sabrina isn't here, but we take a four-seater table anyway, sitting across from one another and waiting as seven o'clock comes and goes. "Do you think she's screwing with us?" I ask. "Just jerking us around?"

"I bet you know a lot about that particular subject," Sabrina says, approaching out of the crowd of students that just walked in. She sits down, smirking triumphantly. "I have to say, I didn't think you would show. I thought I was pushing it with the hundred, but I thought I might as well go balls-out, so to speak." She gives me a little wink, like I'm supposed to laugh at her dirty joke, as if any of this is funny.

"I can't believe you're doing this," I growl, and Sabrina

laughs. "I thought you were nice, but this is wrong, so fucking wrong." I shake my head, still bewildered at how we even ended up in this shitty situation.

"Nice? I'm not the one pretending to be Miss Goody Two-Shoes while fucking my professor. Seriously, I gotta give you some props. You took that dick like a pro. Way better skills than I'd expect from a math nerd." Her voice is harder than I've ever heard, any hint of sweetness dissipating in her catty judgment.

I flush and sputter. "How did I ever think you were a friend?"

"Probably too fuck-drunk to realize what was right in front of your face," she says, shrugging. "Then again, you spent most of the semester ogling Prof here, too lost in his dick to notice anything. I can't believe you were ever passing. Now I know why."

"She earned her grades," Connor says in a low voice. "Every single one of them." I know it's true, but I can see that Sabrina doesn't believe him for a second.

But now she's got Connor in her sights and she dismisses our little back and forth, locking her eyes on him. "All those damn brains, and still not enough to understand that sometimes, that just doesn't fucking matter," Sabrina says, growing very serious. "Let's talk business."

"So, what's the plan?" Connor asks casually.

Sabrina falters a little. I think she expected him to be more rattled than he is. Honestly, I expected him to be more aggressive too, but I'm trusting this is step one of . . . something. "Well, first, those grades of mine . . .

yeah, you're going to do what you need to bring them up. I understand you can't make it obvious, but you're smart. Make it work. I'll need an *A* in your class as the final grade. Understand?"

"Done," Connor says. "And the money?"

She shrugs, as if blackmail isn't a big deal. "Why not? Those pics seemed worth something, and college is fucking expensive. This little exchange"—she points between me, Connor, and herself— "is going to pay for my degree, oh, plus my scholarship, of course. That'll keep me on track with an *A* in your class." She smirks, like she can already count the money.

Connor nods, summarizing. "So, let me get this straight . . . you want one hundred thousand dollars and an *A* you didn't earn, and you'll keep your mouth shut and delete the pictures of Daisy and me? That about right?"

Sabrina grins a sweet smile and nods, looking nothing like the evil bitch she is. If anyone looked over here, they'd probably think me and her were besties who happened to run into a professor on a Thursday night pre-final hang-out. "Yes sir, that's the deal. Take it or I'll go to the dean. I think he'd be real interested in what's been happening between you two." The threat is implicit.

I'm confused, looking between Connor and Sabrina, trying to figure out what he has planned because this seems oddly casual. I don't know that I'd expected him to rage or yell, but something doesn't seem right.

And then I see it, the cocky arrogance Connor is known

for. His shit-eating grin tells me that this is exactly what he planned, whatever this is. He winks at me, and my heart races, desperate to see what he's going to do.

"You know, Sabrina, you really should have thought this through better. Then again, you've shown yourself to be a pretty poor student."

"Who the fuck cares?" Sabrina replies, a little rattled. "Give me the money and you get the pictures. You realize you two were so into it you never even locked the door? Amateurs. I had a feeling what was going on, so I quietly opened the door and slid my phone through."

"Speaking of amateurs, the first rule of blackmail is to have information that your victim doesn't want to share. I'm damn proud to be with this woman."

Connor stands up, grabbing my hand and pulling me to my feet. "Everyone!" he calls out, his voice ringing through the restaurant. Almost everything stops, people wondering what the commotion is about. "Everyone, if you don't know me, I'm Professor Connor Daniels, Math department. And this is Daisy Phillips, my girlfriend."

He pulls me against him, kissing me hard before anyone can react. I resist for half a moment, startled more than anything else, before I melt into his kiss, my hands coming up to pull on the back of his neck, deepening the kiss as our tongues twist and writhe around each other. Distantly, I hear the restaurant cheering, hoots of 'get some, dude' and vague *woohoo*s surrounding us.

"Connor," I whisper when our lips part. "Are you sure this is a good idea?" Though most of the students here probably don't realize what they just saw, there's bound to be a few who recognize me as a fellow student and put two and two together that this isn't exactly okay.

"Never been surer," he replies, stroking my cheek. "Eliminate the variables and solve for what's left. And there was only one variable that counted—you. I love you, Daisy Phillips. I love you, heart and soul."

"I love you too," I repeat, a tear trickling from my right eye. "But what about . . ." I look to Sabrina.

She looks shell-shocked, and I can see the anger turning her face red as she sneers. "Soooo touching, but you know that this will end you, right?"

Connor smirks and tells her, "Maybe, but for you, here's what you get. Zero. Zilch. Not a goddamn fucking thing. I went to the dean and told him everything. He'd like to talk with you about your conduct. Sure, I could be out of a job, but you see, Miss Bowen, blackmail is against the law, and blackmailing a professor for better grades? That's grounds for expulsion too."

Sabrina stutters, "W–what? No!" She looks around wildly as her plan blows up in her face, but I've got to give her credit, she recovers quickly. "I'll deny it. *I have no idea what Professor Daniels is talking about, Dean Michaels.*" She raises her voice, mimicking the innocent tone she thinks will work on the dean. Partnered with the batting lashes and sweet smile, I'll admit that it's a good sell.

Connor laughs and looks past her. "Hey, Nick . . . you get all that?"

A guy I've never seen stands up. "Yep, CD. Got every last word and faux innocent gesture."

"Thanks, man. Can you forward that on to Dean Michaels and send me a copy? He's expecting it." I watch as the guy, obviously a friend of Connor's, taps on his phone and then holds out a thumbs-up sign. Connor turns to Sabrina. "Dean Michaels is expecting you too. Eight A.M. tomorrow morning, Miss Bowen."

And then he takes my hand, leading me out and leaving Sabrina fuming as she yells after us, "I hope you get fired!"

Connor doesn't even react, though the reality is that still could happen. But it feels good to be out in the open, not a dirty little secret but proud to be by my man's side, claiming him and being claimed by him publicly.

There are a few cheers as we leave, but I don't really care. All I care about is the look in Connor's eyes . . . because that's the only thing that counts.

EPILOGUE

CONNOR

*I*t's a beautiful summer day, and normally, I'd be resentful that I'm having to work. But considering all the other ways Dean Michaels could have punished me, I guess teaching summer term isn't all that bad. He'd definitely hinted at worse, but luckily, the *TED Talk* people finally got around to asking me to present, a huge boon for both me and the university, and the timing couldn't have been better. Though I'd lost my shot at tenure, at least for the time being, I'm happy to still have my job. Even if I could've found a better-paying position in the private sector, I like what I do.

Besides, there are benefits. The summer teaching load isn't all that heavy, and it's given Daisy and me time to be together. At least when she's not in class too.

Rolling over in bed, I give Daisy a soft kiss. "Good morning, love."

Daisy stretches and yawns, her natural beauty only enhanced by the messy hair and bare face. I feel like a lucky bastard for seeing her like this, fresh from sleeping in my arms all night. "Good morning. What time is it?"

"Seven thirty," I reply, burying my head in the curve of her neck and kissing the soft skin there gently. "Too late to do what I want with you right now . . . but today's the last day of class."

"Mmm, I know," Daisy moans lightly, pressing her ass back against my hard cock. "It was just last night. Don't you ever get tired?" Her voice is teasing. She already knows the answer but wants me to talk dirty to her. I'm happy to oblige.

"Of that sweet pussy wrapped around my cock while you scream my name? Never," I promise. It's been a few weeks since Daisy moved in, and I'm glad. It just felt natural, after spring semester was over and she was out of the dorms, to have her move in with me. Sure, some people have wondered, but after she turned in a legitimate perfect score on her final from a different professor, none of my colleagues have dared to say a thing. At least, not to my face. Well, except for Nick, of course. He's given me shit, but all his comments have been friendly teasing. Honestly, I think he's a little jealous, but that's okay.

"So, are you driving me to class?" Daisy asks, turning over to look in my eyes. "You know, to wish me good luck?"

I laugh softly, shaking my head. "After a whole summer term of blowing Professor Patel's socks off, you hardly need good luck."

Daisy hums, reaching down to take my cock in hand.

"Mmm . . . speaking of blowing, I know a Professor I'd rather be blowing."

I chuckle, moaning lightly as Daisy kisses down my chest. "And you were wondering if I ever get tired?"

Pausing, her sweet lips just an inch above my cock, she looks up, giving me the naughty smile that only I get to see. "Well, Professor, you've been tutoring me in more than just math . . . and I love every minute of it, but maybe you could critique my new technique?"

She licks at my head, moaning against my skin and driving me wild. "Fuck, Daisy. I love it too, and I love you."

She tries to pull back to say she loves me too. I can see the words in her eyes, but I hold her down, mouth full of my cock. "I know, honey. Now, about that final exam." I smirk, and her eyes light up, happily playing along.

OF COURSE, THERE'S A REASON THAT I WANTED DAISY to go to class on her own this morning, and it had nothing to do with campus life. We've gotten used to the looks, but as long as Daisy isn't in my class, nobody can say a damn thing.

After the dean pulled Sabrina into his office, the investigation was swift considering we had video of her confessing to everything. But she begged forgiveness. The dean was still going to throw her out until Daisy, in a move that surprised me, intervened. My good-hearted

LAUREN LANDISH

girl asked that Sabrina be given another chance . . . if the photos were destroyed. Of course, Sabrina was willing to do that, deleting the file in front of Daisy that very instant. She's still in school, although her plan for avoiding student debt has certainly backfired and her scholarship for next year was revoked. But with no criminal charges filed, she'll figure out something, I'm sure. As long as it has nothing to do with Daisy and me or anything illegal.

But that has nothing to do with my little errand for the morning, pressed in between breakfast and getting to the office to prepare for the final I'm giving at noon.

"It's a beautiful choice, sir," the salesperson comments as I slide the string of pearls over my fingers. I can't help it. The sensation makes my cock stiffen, but I guess that's to be expected. Daisy's pearls have been washed, and I did give her that necklace of a different sort as promised . . . but this is something even more significant, a start of an new heirloom, something permanent and meaningful for us. "Is there anything else?"

"Yes," I reply, shifting over a little. "I'd like them wrapped in satin, if you have it. And I'd like to add something a little bit special to the package. Would you help me over here?"

The salesperson sees what I'm looking at and grins. "A fine choice, sir."

Daisy

"I still can't believe you took summer classes, but I'll see you soon," Arianna says in my ear as I bounce out of

142

the student center where I've been wasting time until four o'clock, when Connor's final ends. "Seriously, I know you love the guy, but studying during summer?"

"You know I've been doing more than studying," I joke, making her laugh. "And the internship . . . how's that?"

"Good! I mean, I'm just working as a front desk receptionist right now, but I'm just glad to have my foot in the door," Ari says, excited. "Hopefully, I can move up to something more hands-on next semester and really start learning. Good part right now, though . . . the eye candy, girl."

"Oh?" I ask, excited for her . . . for both the internship she wanted and that she might have her sights on someone. "Anyone in particular?"

"The CEO," Arianna says, her voice giving away that she's crushing on him. "Remember when I said he was probably just a rich hotshot? He's that, I'm sure, but Oh, my God. You know the M&M slogan, melts in your mouth and not in your hand? I think I want to test that theory on him . . . bet I could get him to melt in my hand, and my mouth. Probably a few other key places too."

I burst out laughing. "Sounds like you're interested in learning *something*, for sure," I tease.

"Yeah, well, he's sexy like it's his job, and I only get to see him for a few seconds a day, but I damn sure get all the eyeful I can during those few seconds."

I grin even though she can't see me. "That sounds just like you. Who knows? Maybe you'll get to see him more.

They'll no doubt bring you back next semester after you knock their socks off."

She sighs dreamily. "Thanks, chica. You're right. I got this."

"That's my girl. When you get back, dinner together, okay?"

"That sounds great. It'll be weird not dorming together this year, but I'll admit that having my own place this summer has been kind of sweet. No one but me to clean up after." I ignore her dig at my tendency to leave my dirty dishes soaking in the sink because it's a battle we've good-naturedly fought more than once already. "And my new digs are right between campus and work, so it's perfect."

"And you can come over to our place anytime." The words feel good on my tongue . . . *our place*. "Connor's going to find himself in charge of a nerd harem," I joke. "Oh, wait, you wouldn't qualify. You're not a nerd."

Arianna laughs. "Nope, but I love nerds. Especially you, girl. I'll see you in a couple of weeks."

"Okay, babe. Bye," I reply, approaching the math building. Bounding up the steps, I see Professor Patel leaving and give him a wave. "Hey, Professor. I'm feeling good after that final."

"You should, Miss Phillips," Patel says, stopping. "It's not official yet, but congratulations on your *A*. It was a pleasure. See you this fall."

I'm even more excited as I nearly run down the hall to Connor's office, closing and making sure to lock the door behind me as soon as I see he's alone, standing at his whiteboard, writing something I can't see. "Hey, Professor, can I talk to you about my grade?" I tease, my voice full of faux-innocent naughtiness.

"Hello, beautiful." He doesn't take my bait, staying serious though he smiles. "I can tell by your smile that you heard about your grade. Patel told me. I'm so proud of you."

I cross the office, barely giving him time to cap his pen before grabbing him by the arms and dragging him to his chair. "Thank you, sir. This good girl needs a reward for all those *long, hard* hours of math," I purr before kissing him. "I can't wait until after dinner."

Connor grins wolfishly. "A reward, you say? Something beyond the *A*? Maybe something a bit *bigger, thicker, harder* . . .?" The return to sexy double-meanings as we tease each other is fun, a hint of our previous dips into being bad together.

He grabs around my waist, pulling me to stand between his spread knees. Holding me in his powerful arms, his lips trail down my neck to the V-neck of my T-shirt, licking and sucking on the mounds of my breasts as he thumbs my nipples through the cotton. It's amazing. Connor's touch can send shivers through my body every time, no matter where we are or what we're doing, but sneaking little trysts in his office has an extra-naughty appeal. I mean, we're in a relationship, and everyone's okay with that . . . but sex in the office is still a no-no. But that's never stopped us before.

I lift my arms to help Connor take my shirt off, gasping

as he doesn't even undo my bra but lifts my right breast out of the cup to consume my nipple, sucking hard and making me cry his name out softly. "Connor, fuck . . . that feels amazing."

"You're amazing," Connor says, switching to my other breast. We know we can't take a ton of time. Every time in his office is truly a 'quickie,' but I've discovered a passion for both the fast and dirty and the slow and loving. Reaching down, I undo his jeans while he lavishes my breasts with his tongue and lips, nipping at my skin when I wrap my hand around his cock and pump him hard and fast.

"Mmm, on the desk," I gasp, letting go of his cock, hurriedly unbuttoning my own jeans and shoving them down my legs to bunch at my ankles. "Hard, baby."

I lie on the desk, just like so many times before as Connor pushes his pants down a little more before lining the tip of his cock up with my wet entrance. He teases me for a few seconds, dragging it up to near my asshole. "Mmm, soon, I'm going to take your virgin ass too, and then all your cherries will be mine . . . mouth, pussy, and your tight little ass. All mine."

The thought is intoxicating. He's fingered my ass before, and while it feels amazing during sex, afterward, I can't help but blush at the dirty things he does to me. I think the innocent blush is part of what he loves about doing it.

I moan, wondering if he's going to push into my tight pucker now, but he just teases me. "I got you something," he groans, voice tight with lust.

"I can feel that," I say with a seductive smile, looking over my shoulder at him.

His cocky grin is all arrogance. "That too, but I meant that." He lifts his chin toward a long, skinny box on the desk, black with a white ribbon tied around it. "Open it."

It's on the tip of my tongue to argue, wanting his cock more than any gift, but I hear the order, and before I know what I'm doing, my hands reach for the box. As I try to untie the bow, Connor slips along my folds, rubbing from my ass to my clit with his cockhead, spreading my cream and his precum all over me, making me sloppy wet with the combination of us. I finally get the bow undone and open the box to find . . . a long chain of rubber beads, pearlized white and gradually getting bigger until the ring on one end.

"What's this?" I ask, already knowing the answer but wanting him to say it. I bite my lip, waiting desperately for his filthy words.

He leans over me, covering me with his hard body and pressing me against the hard wood of the desk, to growl in my ear. "Those are the pearls I'm gonna slip inside your ass, one at a time, bigger and bigger, until you're ready to take my cock in your tight hole. Because when I get that cherry, I'm going to ride you hard, Daisy, and I need you prepared for that. I meant to give them to you tonight, but right now, I want nothing more than to fuck your pussy with them in your ass, filling you so fucking full. Can you do that? Take the pearls in your ass like a good girl?"

147

I whimper but nod, so lost in lust I'm unable to form words.

He lifts off me, slipping the pearls along my pussy to coat them in honey before pressing the smallest one against my ass. "Relax."

I exhale and I feel the pearl slip inside. It feels odd, but good. Connor rubs my clit, and as I buck back, searching for his hand, another pearl slides inside. Or was it two? I can't tell. All I know is I feel full but also empty, my pussy pulsing desperately to be filled too.

"Fuck me, Connor. Please," I beg.

He lines his rock-hard cock up with my pussy, sliding all the way in with one deep thrust. "Mmm . . . you feel so good, satin walls gripping my cock," he growls as he grinds deep inside me. "I could stay inside you forever."

I stifle a cry as he thrusts again. It's fast, deep, and brutal, just what my body needs as Connor hammers my pussy with his cock, both of us pushing the other higher. I squeeze his cock with every thrust, milking him and encouraging him to give me more, to take me higher.

Of course Connor can. He grunts and groans, adding to the heat of our intense fucking as he begins to move the string of pearls in and out of my ass, fucking both my holes. It's like nothing I've ever imagined, so much stimulation as he sometimes thrusts into me with his cock and the pearls at once, sometimes alternating. He keeps me on my toes, literally and figuratively, not knowing what to expect as he pounds me into the desk.

I slap my hand over my mouth, stifling the cries of my

ecstasy so no one in the hallway can hear, even though a part of me wants them to, is turned on that they'll hear my Professor fucking my student pussy and ass.

He speeds up, his cock swelling and making me fight back a scream as my body trembles before exploding in a massive climax that leaves me gasping for breath. I squeeze the desk edge as Connor strangles back a cry before coming hard, his warm seed filling my body and making me tremble again in what I've come to call after-shock orgasms, tears of joy trickling from the corners of my eyes.

When it's over, I sigh happily, totally spent for the moment.

Connor sits in his chair, pulling me into his lap, and I rest my head on his shoulder as he twirls a lock of my black hair around his finger. "Hey, Daisy? I was hoping you could help me with an equation. Think you can take a look?"

I blink, a little surprised, but I nod. "Uhh, you need *my* help?"

He leads me toward the whiteboard. "What do you think?"

I look at the equation, then back at him.

$$C+D=F$$

If it wasn't for the hopeful look in his eyes, I'd probably be lost. Connor plus Daisy equals forever.

"Well, first, we need to solve for the variables. What's the expression for F?" I tease, not wanting to get my hopes up that he means what I think he does. But my heart is transparent to Connor and he knows exactly what I'm thinking.

Connor nods, going over to his desk and getting a small flat box that he brings back before getting on a knee. "I love you. With all that I am, all that I have, all I ever will have. All I can think of is you. Daisy Phillips, will you marry me?"

He opens the box, and inside, I see a beautiful string of pearls, and strung on them, resting precisely in the center, is a diamond ring, sparkling on a bed of white satin.

I swallow and nod as Connor takes out the pearls and pulls the ring from them, making me grin widely. "Yes, Connor! Oh, my God, yes!"

He slips the ring on my finger, and I hold it up, admiring the sparkly diamond that symbolizes so much more than I'd ever dreamed possible. He kisses me, sweet and deep, just like our love.

I pull back, telling him, "But you made a mistake in your equation."

"What?" Connor asks, the arrogant smirk on his face telling me just how clever he thought he was being. "I thought it was pretty good, myself."

"True . . . but like you taught me, you have to identify all your variables precisely," I admonish. I pick up the marker, adding to the equation so that it reads . . . $C+D+1=F$.

Connor's eyes widen in comprehension, and he pulls me

tightly, spinning me around. "As you like to tell me, the answer is still the same. You're mine. Forever. Both of you."

Thank you for reading! You can find Leather and Lace & Silk and Shadows, The Virgin Diaries Books 2 & 3 on Amazon Now!

Continue on for a preview of Dirty Talk.

Join my mailing list and receive 2 FREE ebooks! You'll also be the first to know if new releases, sales, and giveaways.

PREVIEW: DIRTY TALK

DERRICK

*M*y black leather office chair creaks, an annoying little trend it's developed over the past six months that's the primary reason I don't use it in the studio. Admittedly, that's probably for the better because if I had a chair this comfortable in the studio, I'd be too relaxed to really be on point for my shows. Still, it's helpful to have something nice like this office since it's a hell of a big step up from the days when my office was also the station's break room. "All right, hit me. What's on the agenda for today's show?"

My co-star, Susannah, checks her papers, making little checkmarks as she goes through each item. She's an incessant checkmarker, and I have no idea how the fuck she can read her sheets by the end of the day. "The overall theme for today is cheaters, and I've got several emails pulled for that so we can stay on track. We'll field calls, of course, and some will be on topic and some off, like always. I'll try and screen them as best I can, and we should be all set."

I nod, trying to mentally prep myself for another three-hour stint behind the mic, offering music, advice, hope, and sometimes a swift kick in the pants to our listeners. Two years ago, I never would've believed that I'd be known as the 'Love Whisperer' on a radio talk segment called the same thing. Part Howard Stern, part Dr. Phil, part DJ Love Below, I've found a niche that's just . . . unique.

I started out many years ago as a jock, playing football on my high school team with dreams of college ball. A seemingly short derailment after an injury led me to do sports reporting for my high school's news and I fell in love.

After that, my scholarships to play football never came, but it didn't bother me as much as I thought it would. I decided to chase after a sports broadcast degree instead, marrying my passion for football and my love of reporting.

I spent four years after graduation doing daily sports talks from three to six as the afternoon drive-home DJ. It wasn't a big station, just one of the half-dozen stations that existed as an alternative for people who didn't want to listen to corporate pop, hip-hop, or country. It was there I received that fateful call.

Looking back, it's kind of crazy, but a guy had called in bitching and moaning about his wife not understanding his need to follow all these wild superstitions to help his team win.

"I'm telling you D, I went to church and asked God himself. I said, if you can bless the Bandits with a win, I'll show myself

true and wear those ugly ass socks my pastor gave me for Christmas the year before and never wash them again. You know what happened?"

Of course, everyone could figure out what happened. Still, I respectfully told him that I didn't think his unwashed socks were doing a damn thing for his beloved team on the basketball court, but if he didn't put those fuckers in the washing machine, they were sure going to land him in divorce court.

He sighed and eventually gave in when I told him to wash the socks, thank his wife for putting up with his shit, and full-out romance her to bed and do his damndest to make up for his selfish ways.

And that was that. A new show and a new me were born. After a few marketing tweaks, I've been the so-called 'Love Whisperer' for almost a year now, helping people who ask for advice to get the happily ever after they want.

Ironically, I'm single. Funny how that works out, but all the good advice I try to give stems from my parents who were happily married for over forty years before my mom passed. I won't settle for less than the real thing, and I try to advise my listeners to do the same.

And then there's the sex aspect of my job.

Talking about relationships obviously involves discussing sex with people, as that's one of the major areas that cause problems for folks. At first, talking about all the crazy shit people want to do even made me blush a little, but eventually, it's just gotten to be second nature.

Want to talk about how to get your wife to massage your prostate? Can do. Want to talk about how your girl-friend wants you to wear Underoos and call her Mommy? Can do. Want to talk about your husband never washing the dishes, and how you can get him to help? I can do that too.

All-in-one, real relationships at your service. Live from six to nine, five days a week, or available for download on various podcast sites and clip shows on the weekends. Hell of a lot for a guy who figured *making it* would involve becoming the voice of some college football team.

So I want to do a good job. And that means working well with Susannah, who is the control-freak yin to my laissez-faire yang. "Thanks. I know this week's topics from our show planning meeting, but I spaced on tonight's focus."

Susannah nods, unflappable. "No problem. Do you want to scan the emails or just do your thing?"

I smile at her. She already knows the answer. "Same as always, spontaneous. You know that even though I was a Boy Scout, being prepared for this doesn't do us any favors. I sound robotic when I read ahead. First read, real reactions work better and give the listeners knee-jerk common sense."

She shrugs, scribbling on her papers. "I know, just checking."

It's probably one of the reasons we work so well together, our totally different approaches to the show. Joining me from day one, she's the one who keeps our show running behind the scenes and keeps me on track on-air, serving as both producer and co-host. Luckily, her almost anal-retentive penchant for prep totally doesn't come across on the air, where she's the playful, comedic counter to my gruff, tell-it-like-it-is style.

"Then let's rock," I tell her. "Got your drinks ready?"

Susannah nods as we head toward the studio. Settling into my broadcast chair, a much less comfortable but totally silent one, I survey my normal spread of one water, one coffee, and one green tea, one for every hour we're gonna be on the air. With the top of the hour news breaks and spaced out music jams, I've gotten used to using the exactly four minute and thirty second breaks to run next door and drain my bladder if I need to.

Everything ready, we smile and settle in for another show. "Gooooood evening! It's your favorite 'Love Whisperer,' Derrick King here with my lovely assistant, Miss Susannah Jameson. We're ready for an evening of love, sex, betrayal, and lust, if you're willing to share. Our focus tonight is on cheaters and cheating. Are you being cheated on? Maybe *you* are the cheater? Call in and we'll talk."

The red glow from the holding calls is instant, but I traditionally go to an email first so that I can roll right in. "While Susannah is grabbing our first caller, I'll start with an email. Here's one from P. 'Dear Love Whisperer,' it says, 'my husband travels extensively for work, leaving me home and so lonely. I don't know if he's cheating while he's gone, but I always wonder. I've started to develop feelings for my personal trainer, and

I think I'm falling in love with him. What should I do?'
"

I *tsk-tsk* into the microphone, making my displeasure clear. "Well, P, first things first. Your marriage is your priority because you made a vow. For better or worse, remember? It's simple. Talk to your husband. Maybe he's cheating, maybe he isn't. Maybe he's working his ass off so his bored wife can even *have* a trainer and you're looking for excuses to justify your own bad behavior. But talking to him is your first step. You need to explain your feelings and that you need him more than perhaps you need the money. Second, you need to get a life beyond your husband and trainer. I get the sense you need some attention and your trainer is giving it to you, so you think you're in love with him. Newsflash—he's being paid to give you attention. By your husband, it sounds like. That's not a healthy foundation for a relationship even if he is your soulmate, which I doubt."

I sigh and lower my voice a little. I don't want to cut this woman's guts out. I want to help her. "P, let's be honest. A good trainer is going to be personable. They're in a sales profession. They're not going to make it in the industry without either being the best in the world at what they do or having a good personality. And a lot of them have good bodies. Their bodies are their business cards. So it's natural to feel some attraction to your trainer. But that doesn't mean he's going to stick by you. Here's a challenge—tell your trainer you can't pay him for the next three months and see how available he is to just give you his time."

Susannah snickers and hits her mic button. "That's why

I do group yoga classes. Only thing that happens there is sweaty tantric orgies. Ohmm . . . my . . ." Her initial yoga-esque ohm dissolves into a pleasure-induced moan that she fakes exceedingly well.

I roll my eyes, knowing that she does nothing of the sort. "To the point, though, fire your trainer because of your weakness and tell him why. He's a pro. He needs to know that his services were not the reason you're leaving. Next, get a hobby that fulfills you beyond a man and talk to your husband."

I click a button and a sound effect of a cheering audience plays through my headset. It goes on like this for a while, call after call, email after email of helping people.

Well, I hope I'm helping them. They seem to think I am, and I'm certainly giving it my best shot. In between, I mix in music and a hodgepodge of stuff that fits the daily themes. Tonight I've got some Taylor Swift, a little Carrie Underwood, some old-school TLC. I even, as a joke, worked in Bobby Brown at Susannah's insistence.

Coming back from that last one, I see Susannah gesture from her mini-booth and give the airspace over to her, letting her introduce the next caller. "Okay, Susannah's giving me the big foam finger, so what've we got?"

"You wish I had a big finger for you," Susannah teases like she always does on air—it's part of our act. "The next caller would like to discuss some rather incriminating photos she's come across. Apparently, Mr. Right was Mr. Everybody?"

I click the button, taking the call live on-air. "This is the 'Love Whisperer', who am I speaking with?"

The caller stutters, obviously nervous, and in my mind I know I have to treat this one gently. Some of the callers just want to laugh, maybe have their fifteen seconds of fame or get their pound of proverbial flesh by exposing their partner's misdeeds. But there are also callers like this, who I suspect really needs help. "This is Katrina . . . Kat."

Whoa, a first name. And from the sound of it, a real one. She's not making a thing up. I need to lighten the mood a little, or else she's gonna clam up and freak out on me. "Hello, Kitty Kat. What seems to be the problem today?"

I hear her sigh, and it touches me for some reason. "Well . . . I can't believe I actually got through, first of all. I worked up the nerve to dial the numbers but didn't expect an answer. I'm just . . . I don't even know what I am. I'm just a little lost and in need of some advice, I guess." She huffs out a humorless laugh.

I can hear the pain in her voice, mixed with nerves. "Advice? That I can do. That's what I'm here for, in fact. What's going on, Kat?"

"It's my boyfriend, or my soon-to-be ex-boyfriend, I guess. I found out today that he slept with someone else." She sounds like she's found a bit of steel as she speaks this time, and it makes her previous vulnerability all the more touching.

"Ouch," I say, truly wincing at the fresh wound. A day of cheat call? I'm sure the advertisers are rubbing their hands in glee, but I'm feeling for this girl. "I'm so sorry. I know that hurts and it's wrong no matter what. I heard something about compromising pics. Please tell me he didn't send you pics of him screwing someone else?"

She laughs but it's not in humor. "No, I guess that would've been worse, but he had sex with someone kind of Internet famous and she posted faceless pics of them together. But I recognized his . . . uhm . . . his . . ."

Let's just get the schlong out in the open, why don't we? "You recognized his penis? Is that the word you're looking for?"

"Yeah, I guess so," Kat says, her voice cutting through the gap created by the phone line. "He has a mole, so I know it's him."

There's something about her voice, all sweet and breathy that stirs me inside like I rarely have happen. It's not just her tone, either. She's in pain, but she's mad as fuck too, and I want to help her, protect her. She seems innocent, and something deep inside me wants to make her a little bit dirty.

"Okay, first, repeat after me. Penis, dick, cock." I wait, unsure if she'll do it but holding my breath in the hopes that she will.

"Uh, what?"

I feel a small smile come to my lips, and it's my turn to be a little playful. "Penis, dick, cock. Trust me, this is important for you. You can do it, Kitty Kat."

I hear her intake of breath, but she does what I demanded, more clearly than the shyness I expected. "Penis, dick, cock."

"Good girl," I growl into the mic, and through the window connecting our booths, I can see Susannah giving me a raised eyebrow. "Now say . . . I recognized his cock fucking her."

I say a silent prayer of thanks that my radio show is on satellite. I can say whatever I want and the FCC doesn't care.

I can tell Kat is with me now, and her voice is stronger, still sexy as fuck but without the lost kitten loneliness to it. "I recognized his cock fucking her tits."

My own cock twitches a little, and I lean in, smirking. "Ah, so the plot thickens. So Kat, how does it feel to say that?"

She sighs, pulling me back a little. "The words don't bother me. I'm just not used to being on the radio. But saying that about my boyfriend pisses me off. I can't believe he'd do that."

"So, what do you think you should do about it?" I ask, leaning back in my chair and pulling my mic toward me. "Is this a 'talk it through and our relationship will be stronger on the other side of this' type situation, or is this a 'hit the road, motherfucker, and take Miss Slippy-Grippy Tits with you?' Do you want my opinion or do you already know?"

"You're right," Kat says, chuckling and sounding stronger again. "I already know I'm done. He's been a wham-bam-doesn't even say thank you, ma'am guy all along, and I've been hanging on because I didn't think I deserved better. But I don't deserve this. I'm better off alone."

Whoa, now, only half right there, Kat with the sexy voice. "You don't deserve this. You should have someone who treats you so well you never question their love, their commitment to you. Everyone deserves that. Hey, Kitty Kat? One more thing. Can you say 'cock' for me one more time? Just for . . . entertainment."

I'm pushing the line here, both for her and for the show, but I ask her to do it anyway because I want, no need, to hear her say it.

She laughs, her voice lighter even as I know the serious conversation had to hurt. "Of course, Love Whisperer. Anything for you. You ready? Cock." She draws the word out, the k a bit harsher, and I can hear the sass, almost an invitation, as she speaks.

"Ooh, thanks so much, Kitty Kat. Hold on the line just a second." My cock is now fully hard in my pants, and I'm not sure if my upcoming bathroom break is going to be to piss or to take care of that.

I click some buttons, sending the show to a song, Shaggy's *It Wasn't Me* coming over the airwaves to keep the cheating theme rolling. "Susannah?"

"Yeah?"

"Handle the next call or so after the commercial break," I tell her. "Pick something . . . funny after that one."

"Gotcha," Susannah says, and I'm glad she's able to handle things like that. It's part of our system too that when I get a call that needs more than on-air can handle, she fills the gap. Usually with less serious questions or listener stories that always make for great laughs.

Checking my board, I click the line back, glad that Susannah can't hear me now. "Kat? You still there?"

"Yes?" she says, and I feel another little thrill go down my cock just at her word. God, this woman's got a sexy voice, soft and sweet with a little undercurrent of sassiness . . . or maybe I really, really need to get laid.

"Hey, it's Derrick. I just wanted to say thanks for being such a good sport with all of that."

"No problem," she says as I make a picture in my head of her. I can't fill in the details, but I definitely want to. "Thanks for helping me realize I need to walk away. I already knew it, but some inspiration never hurts."

"I really would like to hear the rest of the story if you don't mind calling me back. I want to hear how he grovels when he finds out what he's lost. Would you call me?"

I don't know what I'm doing. This is so not like me. I never talk to the callers after they're on air unless I think they're going to hurt themselves or others, and I certainly never invite them to call back. But something about her voice calls to me like a siren. I just hope she's not pulling me into the rocky shore to crash.

"You mean the show?" Kat asks, uncertain and confused. "Like . . . I dunno, like a guest or something?"

"Well, probably not, to be honest," I reply, crossing my fingers even as my cock says I need to take this risk. "We'll be done with the cheating theme tonight and it probably won't come back up for a couple of weeks. I meant . . . call me. I want to make sure you're okay afterward and standing strong."

"Okay."

Before she can take it back, I rattle off my personal cell number to her, half of my brain telling me this is brilliant and the other half saying it's the stupidest thing I've ever done. I might not have the FCC looking over my shoulder, but the satellite network is and my advertisers for damn sure are. Still . . . "Got it?"

"I've got it," Kat says. "I'll get back to you after I break up with Kevin. It's been a weird night and I guess it's going to get even weirder. Guess I gotta go tell Kevin his dick busted him on the internet and he can get fucked elsewhere . . . permanently. I can do this."

"Damn right, you can," I tell her. "You can do this, Kitty Kat. Remember, you deserve better. I'll be waiting for your report."

Kat laughs and we hang up. I don't know what just happened but my body feels light, bubbly inside as I take a big breath to get ready for the next segment of tonight's show.

Get the full book here.

facebook.com/lauren.landish

twitter.com/laurenlandish

instagram.com/lauren_landish

17380631R00094

Printed in Great Britain
by Amazon